LET YOUR HAIR DOWN

RACHEL LACEY

Let Your Hair Down
Copyright © 2019 by Rachel Lacey
Ebook ISBN: 9781641971003
POD ISBN: 9781088708545
Cover Design © Letitia Hasser, Romantic Book Affairs

NYLA Publishing
121 W 27th St., Suite 1201, New York, NY 10001
http://www.nyliterary.com

LET YOUR HAIR DOWN

1

---

*R*uby Keller crept past a row of ornate marble statues into the gardens beyond. Her heels clicked against stone pavers as she followed a path leading away from the Langdon family estate. Behind her, the wedding reception was in full swing, music and laughter drifting on the air, as rich as the scent of the rosebushes blooming on either side of the path.

She wasn't running away from her best friend's wedding. On the contrary, Elle and Theo's wedding was by far the most beautiful and amazing event she'd ever attended, held at this beautiful estate just outside London, but there were drawbacks to being here without a date. Ruby was accustomed to flying solo at events. It usually didn't faze her. But usually she had her best friends by her side. Now, Elle was married, and Megan was here with her boyfriend, Jake, and they were adorably, disgustingly in love.

For the last half hour, Ruby had fought off the advances of an obnoxiously drunk man named Ellis who couldn't seem to take a hint, not even when she'd pointedly turned to her cell phone and begun scrolling through her social media while he droned on about stock portfolios and dividends. So, when he went to the bar for another drink, Ruby decided to make herself scarce.

She was officially peopled out for the night and hoping to find some peace and quiet here in the gardens. Just for a little while. Then, she'd be a good maid of honor and go back inside to join the party. But, honestly, events like this were exhausting for an introvert.

"Ruby? Are you out here?"

Ellis's deep voice echoed through the garden. It was a shame he was such an ass because he had a sexy voice, and she'd always had a thing for British accents. He wasn't hard to look at either. But he was obnoxious to the point it bordered on harassment. She'd already told him she wasn't interested— several times—and yet, here he was. She stepped off the stone path, walking between two rows of rosebushes.

"I saw you come out here and thought you might like company," he called.

You thought wrong, buddy.

She extended her middle finger in his general direction as she ducked behind a rosebush, bending awkwardly in her floor-length satin dress. There was a sharp tug at her hair, and she reared back with a gasp, right hand raised reflexively in case she needed to defend herself, but no one was there. She was alone, deep in the garden away from the lighted path, her hair snagged on a rosebush.

Well, this was embarrassing. She tipped her head forward, attempting to tug free, but to no avail. Her glasses slid off her nose and tumbled to the ground, out of reach. Ruby exhaled in frustration as she reached behind her head, pricking her finger on a thorn in the process.

"For crying out loud," she muttered. Her fingers encountered more thorns…and more hair. Her meticulously constructed up-do was now engaged in a tug-of-war with the rosebush, and her hair seemed to be losing.

"You look like you could use a hand," a man said from

behind her.

She tensed, half-blind without her glasses and unable to turn around, stuck in a ridiculous crouch lest she rip her hair out by the roots. But this voice—while still deep, masculine, and British—was different. Softer. Kinder. Not Ellis. And she really could use a hand.

"You could say that," she said.

"Hold still," the man said, and a moment later, she felt a gentle tug at the back of her head and fingers poking through her hair. "Let me know if I'm hurting you. It's tangled pretty badly back here."

"It's fine," she said, wincing slightly. "Do what you need to do."

"Almost got it," he said.

Ruby rested her palms on her thighs, attempting to balance in her awkward position. Her rescuer had a nice voice, rich and soothing. He sounded young, and yeah, she was still digging the British accent.

"You're free," he announced.

"Thank you," she breathed, straightening to her full height. One hand went automatically into her hair, which felt like a disheveled mess. The man in front of her was tall and slim, with dark hair and wearing a black tux, like nearly every other man in attendance tonight. That was about all she could tell without her glasses. "I really appreciate it."

"Happy to help," he said, extending a hand in her direction. "Flynn Bowen."

She took it and shook, impressed by the strength of his grasp. "Ruby Keller."

"A pleasure to meet you, Ruby." He leaned forward, his voice dropping conspiratorially. "So, who are you hiding from out here?"

"Excuse me?" She crouched, feeling around for her glasses. Her fingers closed over them, and she slipped them onto her face, standing to face Flynn. And *whoa*. She blinked, attempting

3

to school her expression, because he was hot…in an adorable sort of way. His dark hair was slightly longer than what seemed to be the acceptable "dress code" for the other men here tonight. An unruly lock had fallen over his forehead. His eyes were crinkled in a friendly smile, sparkling with humor.

"See, I was already out here…also hiding," he said with a wink. "My entire family is in there. The Bowens are longtime friends of the Langdons. My parents, brother, sisters, and all their spouses are here tonight. I'm the youngest of five," he explained. "And the only single one. My mother won't stop trying to introduce me to every available woman in the ballroom, so I came out to wander the gardens. And then I saw you sneaking off into the bushes."

"I guess I'm out here for similar reasons," she told him as she attempted to smooth over what remained of her hairdo. "No family here, though, but I'm the only single one left in my group of friends. I'm surprised your mother didn't already introduce us."

"I expect she would have if she knew you," Flynn said, his easy smile never faltering. "But alas, you're American, so I think she might consider you a lost cause."

"She doesn't want you to date an American?" Ruby asked.

"Oh, nothing like that. It's just, I imagine you're only here for the wedding and will be flying home soon after. My mother isn't exactly trying to find me a one-night stand." His grin widened.

Ruby laughed. Flynn's exuberance was infectious. "Well, she'd be right, I guess. I'm sticking around for a week or so to do some sightseeing, but then I'll be flying back to Virginia."

"Really?" Flynn gestured for her to follow him toward a bench on the main path. "Where are you planning to visit?"

"That's the thing." Her body buzzed with a mixture of excitement and nerves. "I haven't made any plans. I'm just going to…see what happens."

"How intriguing." Flynn's eyebrows rose. "A woman with a

4

sense of adventure. I like that."

"If you only knew." She shook her head, feeling what remained of her bun sliding around loosely. "This is so unlike me. I'm an over-planner. I have a spreadsheet for…well, everything."

"Define everything," Flynn said, his gaze locked on hers, intense, but not in an alarming way, more like he was hanging on her every word.

"I have a spreadsheet to help me manage all my spreadsheets."

Flynn laughed, resting a hand on her shoulder. "That is unusual, I'll admit."

She grinned. "I'm an unusual woman, what can I say?"

"I like it. Tell me more." He sat on the bench, patting the empty spot beside him.

She sat, feeling a hundred times lighter than she had a few minutes ago. "Do you want the short version or the long version?"

"Ruby, there you are!" Ellis came around a bend in the path, beelining toward her. He stopped in front of the bench with a slight frown. "Who are you?"

"Flynn Bowen," Flynn said. "And you are?"

"Ellis Mayberry," he announced with an air of self-importance. "Ruby and I were just about to dance. Weren't we, Ruby?"

"Actually, you asked, and I said I wasn't in the mood," she told him, letting her voice fall flat in annoyance.

"Well, I…" Ellis gaped, seemingly—*finally*—at a loss for words. "What happened to your hair?"

"I decided to try a new look," she said, reaching up to touch the side of her head. "What do you think?"

Ellis stared at her, his mouth opening and closing in silent confusion.

"I think Ruby's hair looks rather lovely this way," Flynn said. "Don't you?"

"Yes, of course," Ellis stammered.

"Well, nice meeting you," Flynn said pointedly.

"Likewise, I'm sure," Ellis muttered before turning and walking off in the direction of the estate.

"Is that wanker the reason you were hiding behind a rose-bush when I found you?" Flynn asked, his tone a mixture of humor and annoyance.

"Yes. Does my hair look that terrible?"

"Not at all." Flynn gave her a discerning look. "Although it does look a bit like you and I were going at it behind that rosebush."

"Now who's a wanker?" she teased, ridiculously charmed by his accent.

"Never," he deadpanned.

"My hair's a total mess. I can tell." She patted the back of her head, coming out with a bobby pin…and a thorn. "I'm going to take it down."

"I'll help if you like," he offered, reaching over to tug another pin out of her hair. And since there were about a million more where that came from, she agreed.

"Thank you."

"So, to answer your question before we were so rudely interrupted, I'd like the long version."

"What?" She set a bobby pin in the growing pile on the bench between them.

"You were about to tell me the story behind your adventure here in London and why you've always played it safe before."

"Oh, that." She glanced over at Flynn. "The long version, huh?"

"I think we have time for it while we pull out all these pins." He held one up for emphasis.

"I have primary immunodeficiency," she told him. "I couldn't be around other kids much when I was growing up, because of my faulty immune system, and even so, I was sick a lot. My mom homeschooled me for most of my childhood."

"That must have been very difficult for you." Flynn set a pin on the pile and reached over to give her hand a squeeze.

"I received a bone marrow transplant from my sister when I was seventeen, and I've been mostly as good as new since, although I still have to be careful. But the point of the story is that I spent my childhood locked away safe and bored in my bedroom. I guess it made me cautious. I tend to overanalyze things to death before making a decision, and, you know…the spreadsheets."

"Lots of spreadsheets," Flynn repeated with a nod.

"I'm that person who takes her laptop with her everywhere she goes."

"I see you left it behind tonight," he commented with a smile.

"I left it at home." She sucked in a deep breath and blew it out. "I've never traveled outside of the United States before, and I'm ready to have the adventure of a lifetime, all by myself, no laptop to hide behind."

Flynn tugged another pin out of her hair, his gaze catching hers in the muted light of the garden. "That is one of the most fascinating and brave stories I've ever heard."

"It's not," she protested. A section of her hair tumbled down her back as she removed another pin. "I'm just taking a vacation. Millions of people do it every day."

"Not like this." He pointed a finger at her. "You said it yourself. This is going to be the adventure of a lifetime."

"Well, I hope it will be. Honestly, it's pretty intimidating now that I'm here. I mean, I've been so caught up in wedding activities, I haven't really had a chance to think about what I'll do tomorrow when it's all over."

"Hence the adventure."

"Yes. I've got a hotel booked in London for the next few nights, but beyond that…who knows?"

"Would you like a few suggestions?" he asked.

"I'd love some, actually."

"I assume you know all the main tourist attractions, but do you enjoy theater? The West End is, in my opinion, superior even to Broadway. You can find anything you're interested in, musical, comedy, opera."

"Theater." Ruby felt a flutter of joy in her chest. "I've never been to a Broadway show. In fact, the only theater I've ever seen were the plays Elle was in back in high school."

"Elle who just married Theo?" Flynn's eyebrow went up.

"The very one. She considered being an actress after high school, although that obviously didn't work out. But yeah, I think I'd love to go to the theater." Her hair tumbled loose over her shoulders, and while she usually didn't like it, tonight it didn't feel half bad, shielding her from the cool September breeze.

"The National Gallery has some amazing artwork, da Vinci, Rembrandt. And you absolutely must visit Hampstead Heath. It has the most amazing views of London. Then there's Oxford Street if you enjoy shopping, and Camden Market has just about every cuisine you could imagine."

"Wow," she breathed, completely taken with every idea he'd just put in her head.

"You mentioned that you wanted to take this adventure on your own, but if you're interested in a tour guide, I'd be happy to show you around London tomorrow."

"Oh, I don't know..." She liked Flynn a lot, but she'd planned to do this on her own. And honestly, they'd just met. She didn't know a thing about him. It would be crazy to let him be her tour guide tomorrow. Then again, wasn't the point of this trip go to with the flow, to do the unexpected, even if it was a little bit risky?

∼

Flynn Bowen couldn't remember ever feeling so enchanted by someone he'd just met. He tugged another pin out of Ruby's hair, watching as it spilled in a dark waterfall down her back. And he found himself irrationally hoping she would take him up on his offer.

She stared at him from behind black-rimmed glasses, her pretty pink lips pursed in thought. "Not sure it's wise to let a total stranger show me around London, although it *would* be adventurous."

"You and I are strangers, but we have a mutual friend," he told her. "Theo and I have known each other our whole lives. We attended the same primary and secondary school, although I was a few years behind him."

"So, the Earl of Highcastle will vouch for your character. That's what you're telling me?" She gave him a grin that made her eyes crinkle at the corners.

"Essentially, yes," he told her with a smile of his own.

"You don't have anything else to do tomorrow?" she asked.

"Not tomorrow, as it's Sunday, but I do have business in Wales on Monday."

"What do you do for a living?"

He leaned back, staring into the fountain in front of them. "A better question might be, what *don't* I do?"

"I…don't know what that means."

"It means I've tried a number of positions within the family business, but none seem to have been the right fit." He watched the water as it splashed into the basin of the fountain, only to be sucked back up through the plumbing and begin its journey all over again. That was how he felt most of the time. One of these days, he would find the right position within the company, the one that would launch him right over the edge and out of this holding pattern.

In the meantime, he needed to dedicate himself one hundred percent to his upcoming assignment in Dubai. His parents had taken a chance on him, allowing him to oversee the construction of what would become one of Exeter Hotels' largest locations, and he couldn't let them down.

"I think that happens to a lot of us." Ruby set the last pin on the bench between them and ran her fingers through her hair, smoothing out the bumps and waves. "In fact, Elle, Megan, and I had all been bouncing between jobs until we won that magazine contest last year."

"You won a magazine contest?"

She nodded. "To manage Rosemont Castle. It's how we met Theo." She gestured toward the estate, where Theo was inside, dancing with his new bride.

"Ah."

"Does it look okay?" she asked, tugging at a strand of her hair.

"You look beautiful." He studied her with a smile. "I didn't get a good look at you before your run-in with the rosebush, but I think I might prefer it down."

"Really? I never wear it down."

"No? That's a shame. You have lovely hair."

"I can't stand when it gets in my face."

"May I?" He picked up a pin and gestured to her hair.

"You want to do my hair for me?" she asked, amusement and surprise mixing in her tone.

"I have three sisters." He lifted the hair away from the left side of her face and secured it with several pins, then did the same on the other side.

"Three sisters?"

"I told you I'm the youngest of five. There." He sat back and surveyed his work. "Not bad, if I do say so myself."

Ruby reached up to touch her new hairdo. "I think I like it. I might change my mind when I see myself in a mirror, though."

He lifted his hands in front of him. "I'll take no offense if you hate it. Shall we go find a mirror, then?"

"I suppose I've hidden out here in the gardens long enough." She stood, smoothing her hands over the front of her dress. "It's been nice chatting with you, though."

"Do you really not want to dance, or did you just not want

to dance with Ellis?" he asked, holding out his elbow.

She slipped her hand through it with a small smile. "So polite. I'm not much of a dancer, I'm afraid, but my objection was mainly to dancing with Ellis."

"In that case, after you freshen up, would you care to dance?" He gave her his most charming smile.

"I'd love to." Her eyes twinkled in the moonlight.

"Excellent." They walked into the ballroom, arm-in-arm. The band was playing an upbeat tune at one end of the room, and the dance floor was packed. At the center, he could see the bride and groom. He nodded toward them. "They look like they're having a good time."

"They sure do." Ruby's face lit with a smile, and Flynn's breath caught in his throat. "What?" she asked.

"I just got my first look at you in actual light, and I had no idea I'd been sitting outside with the prettiest woman at the party." He nudged her shoulder playfully. Ruby scoffed at his compliment, but he wasn't joking, not this time. She was lovely, with her dark hair cascading over her shoulders, pinned back to accent her heart-shaped face and those rich chocolate eyes shining behind her glasses. Ruby wore a floor-length pink dress—a bridesmaid's dress—and it hugged her petite frame just right.

"I'm going to the ladies' room. I'll be right back."

"I'll be waiting." He turned toward the bar, only to see his mother waving him over.

"Flynn," she called. "There you are."

And he felt a bit like Ruby had in the garden when Ellis Mayberry caught up with them, because there was a woman standing beside his mother, a blonde in a knee-length black dress smiling shyly in his direction.

"Darling, this is Rebecca Creekmore," his mother said. "Rebecca, this is my son, Flynn."

He glanced over his shoulder in the direction Ruby had gone. This time, it would be her turn to save him.

2

_____

Ruby stood in front of the mirror in the bathroom, one hand in her hair as she turned to the side, surveying her reflection. She hardly recognized the woman staring back at her. Somehow, Flynn had managed to salvage her ruined hairdo and turn it into something kind of beautiful. She didn't usually like how her hair looked when it was down, but the way he'd tucked the sides back really worked, at least with this dress. It was a different look for her, but then again, this week was all about trying new things.

Lots of new things.

The flush she saw in her cheeks wasn't due to the makeup the artist had carefully applied earlier that day. It wasn't even embarrassment over all the various ways her evening had gone wrong so far. It was excitement, a kind of excitement she hadn't felt in too long to remember. The rest of the reception should be a lot more fun now that she had Flynn to hang out with. And tomorrow, she would begin her uncharted adventure in London.

"Whoa," Megan said, appearing in the mirror behind Ruby. "You took your hair down!"

"I had a run-in with a rosebush. I had no choice."

"Well, I love it." Megan walked up to stand beside her, wearing a floor-length rose satin dress identical to Ruby's, as Elle had made them both her maids of honor. "I think I might like it better than your up-do."

"Really?"

"Really." Megan grinned at her in the mirror. The scar that ran down the left side of her face was barely visible tonight beneath her makeup, but it wrinkled slightly when she smiled, a permanent reminder of the car accident they'd been in together a year ago.

"Don't laugh, but I met this guy in the garden, and we really hit it off. He even offered to show me around London tomorrow."

Megan's eyebrows crawled up her forehead. "What? Who? Do we know him? I told you that you could tag along with me and Jake."

"No way. I'm not playing third wheel to you two lovebirds, and besides, I want to do this on my own anyway. I really like Flynn, but I think I'm going to turn him down."

"Well, let's not be hasty," Megan said, shifting gears. "Tell me more about him. What's he like? What do we know about him?"

"He's a friend of Theo's," Ruby told her. "Apparently, their families go way back. He's very nice, funny too."

"You know what? I think it sounds exciting. You should go." Megan pulled out a lipstick from her bag, pursing her lips as she reapplied it. "You did say this week was about having a grand adventure, right?"

Ruby rolled her eyes, then pulled out her own lipstick. She never fussed with her appearance in front of the mirror. But she didn't attend an earl's wedding every day either. Surely that was the reason she was unnaturally obsessed with her appearance tonight. "This adventure is about me, not a man."

"And sometimes," Megan said as she led the way out of the

bathroom, "a man can be part of your adventure. It doesn't make it any less yours."

Ruby was still stewing on that bit of advice as she made her way toward the bar where Flynn stood chatting…with another woman. She was about Ruby's age, a pretty blonde who was currently leaned against the bar in a way that accentuated her cleavage, staring at Flynn like he'd just told her she was the most beautiful woman in the world.

Ruby faltered, heat rising in her cheeks as her stomach dropped. While she'd been in the bathroom, gushing about Flynn to Megan and letting her halfway convince Ruby to accept his offer, he'd been out here finding a new woman to flirt with in her absence.

Maybe Ruby ought to turn the tables on him and find a woman to flirt with too—hey, there were certain advantages to being bisexual—but that wasn't really her style. And honestly, tonight she only had eyes for Flynn. He glanced over, and their eyes locked. Before she could decide what to do, he was waving her over.

But Ruby stayed right where she was, because…nope. She had no desire to hang around while Flynn flirted with someone else. She'd spent enough of the last year as a third wheel to Elle and Theo, and then Megan and Jake. No, thank you. At least she'd realized Flynn was a player before she spent any more time with him.

Then she noticed another woman talking to the blonde, an older woman with dark hair pulled back into a sleek twist and wearing an impeccably styled floor-length black dress. She had to be Flynn's mother. There was no denying the resemblance between them. Which meant the blonde was probably someone his mom had brought over for him to meet. And, now that she was really paying attention, the look Flynn was giving her was more of a plea.

Hoping like hell she had an accurate read on the situation and wasn't about to make a fool of herself, she sucked in a deep breath and walked over to them, stopping beside him. "Hi."

He gave her a grateful smile. "Ruby, this is my mother, Nancy, and that's Rebecca Creekmore, who's an old classmate of Theo's." He gestured to the blonde before turning toward his mom. "And this is Ruby Keller. She's a friend of the bride. We met in the gardens a little while ago."

"How lovely," Flynn's mother said, extending a hand in Ruby's direction, her accent crisp and refined. "A pleasure to meet you, Ruby."

"Likewise," Ruby told her with a polite smile. Her hair tickled her shoulders, as unfamiliar as the rest of her evening, and she wasn't sure how she felt about any of it. Her arrival seemed to have interrupted whatever conversation had been flowing between Flynn, his mom, and Rebecca, who quickly excused herself to rejoin her friends. Flynn's mother followed soon after, having spotted a business associate she wanted to greet.

"Sorry about that," Flynn said, eyes twinkling as they locked on hers. "But thanks for saving me from my mother's latest attempt at matchmaking."

Ruby's stomach got tingly and warm, like it had received an electrical surge. "Happy to help."

"So, would you like to dance?"

"I'd love to."

He took her hand and led her onto the dance floor. The ballroom in the Langdon estate was ornately decorated with a glittering chandelier suspended above the dance floor, casting everyone in warm, muted light, almost as if they were glowing. Flynn led her to a quiet corner, his hands in hers as they began moving to the beat. The band was playing an up-tempo tune that Ruby wasn't familiar with.

She wasn't much of a dancer and was glad Flynn had chosen an out-of-the-way part of the dance floor for them. He moved with the ease of someone who was one-hundred-percent comfortable with himself and his surroundings. He'd probably attended countless events like this one, maybe even other events here at the Langdon estate. Considering that his family were old friends of the Langdons, Flynn probably came from money and social standing.

Occasionally, he took her hand to give her a twirl or guide her in a certain direction as they danced. He'd taken off his tuxedo jacket, and she caught glimpses of his trim, muscular frame beneath his white dress shirt. She couldn't take her eyes off him, and she wasn't the only one. She caught other women watching him too, although his attention never strayed from her.

They danced together through several upbeat songs before the music slowed. Flynn took her hand, gently drawing her closer. "This okay?" he asked as his hands drifted to her hips, barely touching her as he waited for her response.

"Mm hmm," she said, as turned on by the feather-light graze of his fingertips as she was by his manners. At her affirmation, his grip on her waist became more firm. His fingers warmed her skin through the satin of her dress. She rested her hands on his shoulders, settling against him. This close, she could smell his aftershave, something fresh and minty, faint enough not to be annoying, but present enough to make him smell nice. "So, you live in London?" she asked as they swayed to the music.

"I do," he confirmed.

"And do you have your own place in the city?" She couldn't quite picture him living in some mansion with his parents, but maybe he did. Rich people did that sometimes, didn't they?

"Yes." Humor laced his tone. "My sister Genevieve still lives with our parents, but not for long. She's getting married in the spring. Hence the reason my mother is so keen to set me up with every available woman who crosses her path."

She and Flynn spent the next hour or so dancing, and Ruby couldn't remember the last time she'd had so much fun. Maybe it was the atmosphere in the ballroom, where everything seemed to sparkle with money and importance. Maybe it was the way her hair swung loosely over her shoulders, or the promise of the week ahead and her make-it-up-as-she-went adventure. Maybe it was the man in front of her, who made her laugh as much as he filled her with a sizzling kind of attraction she hadn't felt in years.

All of those things usually made her anxious. The need for carefully planned structure usually got the better of her. She couldn't even blame tonight's carefree attitude on too much alcohol. She'd only had a few sips of wine here and there. Tonight, she was drunk on life and the promise of adventure.

Eventually, they made their way toward the bar for a drink. Ruby's toes and the arches of her feet ached from the heels she was unaccustomed to wearing, a discomfort she would happily endure tonight for the chance to dress up and celebrate her friend's wedding.

"Ruby!"

She turned to see Elle hurrying toward her, her princess-style wedding dress swirling around her ankles. The tiara on her head was a Langdon family heirloom that Elle herself had helped locate after Theo's grandfather hid it for "safekeeping" before his death.

Ruby excused herself as Flynn walked ahead to the bar to get their drinks, meeting Elle halfway across the room. "How does it feel wearing that tonight?"

Elle reached up to touch the diamond and pearl crusted piece. "Like I'm living someone else's life."

"Well, Mrs. Langdon, you'd better get used to it, because this is your life now." Ruby gave her friend an impromptu hug. "I'm so happy for you, I could cry."

"Don't you dare," Elle warned. "We spent way too much time on our hair and makeup today to ruin them. Speaking of which, what happened to your hair?"

"It got caught in a rosebush."

"Ouch," Elle said. "But I actually really like this. You should wear it down more often. Anyway, the reason I came looking for you is…who's the guy?"

Ruby glanced over her shoulder at Flynn, who was talking with a couple at the bar. "Flynn Bowen. He's a friend of Theo's."

Elle pursed her lips. "The name is vaguely familiar. You guys looked like you were having so much fun on the dance floor. Do you like him?"

"I do. He's really fun to be around. In fact, he offered to show me around London tomorrow, and I'm considering taking him up on it."

Elle's eyes went comically round. "Whoa, Ruby, that is so unlike you. And also really awesome. Want me to ask Theo about him for you? Make sure he's not a creep?"

Ruby laughed. "Sure, but I don't think he would be here if he was a creep."

"You might be surprised. Money and class dominated a lot of the guest list, and those aren't always good indicators of decency."

Ruby thought of Ellis. "That's true. Okay, ask Theo."

"Will do." Elle gave her another hug before heading across the ballroom in search of her new husband.

Ruby looked around for Flynn and spotted him walking toward her with a glass of wine in each hand. She'd spent hours now debating whether to take him up on his offer. The reception was almost over. It was time to make up her mind, so…if Theo vouched for him, she'd say yes. No more second-guessing herself. She'd come to London to have an unscripted adventure, and hopefully Flynn would be an exciting new part of it. He stopped beside her, handing her a glass of wine.

"Thanks," she told him, bringing it to her lips for a sip.

"My pleasure."

"Ladies and gentlemen, may I have your attention, please," the bandleader called over his microphone. "At this time, we ask you all to please join us for the bride and groom's final dance of the evening."

She and Flynn followed the rest of the guests as they formed a circle around the dance floor to watch the last dance. Elle and Theo walked out, looking radiantly in love as they began to dance. Ruby pressed a hand against her chest, blinking back happy tears. Megan squeezed in beside her, and they wrapped their arms around each other.

When the song ended, Elle headed straight for them, joining Ruby and Megan in a group hug. They clung to each other for a long moment, all of them teary-eyed by the time they pulled away. Before Elle left to rejoin her husband, she whispered in Ruby's ear, "Theo says Flynn is a great guy. Go for it."

So, Ruby sucked in a decisive breath as she turned toward Flynn. "I'd love for you to show me around London tomorrow."

~

FLYNN AND RUBY STROLLED THROUGH THE GARDEN AS THEY finished their wine. The wedding reception had just ended, and soon they'd be heading up to their respective rooms.

"So, what would you like to do tomorrow?" he asked, thrilled that she'd agreed to spend the day with him. Now, he wanted to make sure she had an amazing experience that set the tone for the rest of her vacation. This trip was a big deal for her, and he was honored to be a part of her adventure, however small.

Ruby pressed a finger against her lips, drawing his eyes to the sheen of her lipstick in the lamplight, the way her teeth pressed against her fingertip, sending a burst of heat through his system. "I should probably start with something touristy and then I have to admit, I'm pretty smitten with your idea of going to the theater to see a show. I really want to do that. Except—" She paused, sucking her bottom lip between her teeth and further muddling his brain. "—I don't have anything to wear."

"I'm sure you've got something that would work. The theater's not as formal as you might think, but if you're looking for an excuse to go shopping, you've come to the right place. London has some of the best shopping in the world, you know."

Ruby gulped, her gaze darting to his. "That does sound fun. We could go shopping and then to the theater. Wait, you're a guy. You don't want to go shopping with me."

"On the contrary." He gave her hand a squeeze. "I do." Ruby wouldn't be a fussy shopper, he could tell. In fact, he had a feeling she rarely splurged on herself, and he wanted to be the one who helped her find something stunning to wear for her night on the town.

"You're full of it, Flynn Bowen," she said, doubting his sincerity.

"I am, no doubt," he agreed. "But I'm truly looking forward to taking you shopping tomorrow. I think we'll have a wonderful day together."

"I think so too." She looked up at him with a sweet smile.

"I'm sorry you had to deal with that wanker earlier, but I'm awfully glad I bumped into you out here."

Her smile widened. "Same, on both counts. I guess it all worked out. There's an Ellis at every party, but the Flynn's are much rarer."

Her words landed on a soft spot in his chest that was tender from the judgment of his family over his inability to launch his career. He rubbed at it absently, marveling at the warmth traveling through him at the compliment. "Thank you."

His fingers tightened around hers, and before he could second guess himself, he leaned forward, pausing to hover over her lips as he looked into her eyes, seeking permission. In their chocolate depths, he saw the same lust currently racing through his system. He pressed his lips to hers, just a quick brush of skin on skin.

Ruby's lips were warm and soft, glossy with lipstick that left his own lips feeling slick and tasting faintly of candy. She exhaled against his mouth, a puff of warm air that blew away his resolve.

His eyes slid shut as he kissed her again, firmer this time, mouths moving together as he dropped his hand to her waist, drawing her closer. A little moan escaped her lips, and Flynn felt like he could probably kiss Ruby forever and never get enough. She was soft and sweet, but also strong and passionate and smart.

He lifted his head, grinning down at her as his heart tapped out a happy rhythm inside his chest. "I'll see you tomorrow, then."

She blinked, her eyes dazed and glazed with lust, before smiling back at him. "Tomorrow."

3

---

*R*uby folded her bridesmaid dress and tucked it inside one of her packing cubes. Her suitcase was neat and orderly, but her brain was not. It was spinning so fast she felt dizzy. She would be meeting Flynn out front in fifteen minutes, and she hadn't planned a single moment of the day to come. Or the day after. Or the day after that.

There wasn't a spreadsheet to prepare her for the aftereffects of that kiss, which left her stomach feeling like it contained a hurricane. A very warm, welcome hurricane. What if Flynn expected her to spend the night with him after their day together in London? Did she want that? She didn't *not* want it. But while he definitely lit her up in a way she hadn't felt in a long time, she wasn't sure she was ready to move that fast with him either.

Today was about having fun and seeing London, although she certainly wouldn't object to another kiss if the opportunity presented. It was time to say farewell to the Langdon estate— and her friends—and embark on the next leg of her adventure. She had a hotel booked in London, but other than that, her itinerary was one hundred percent up in the air.

She zipped her suitcase and pressed a hand against her

stomach. This had to be what it felt like when you jumped out of an airplane, that time of freefall before the parachute opened. Ruby never jumped without a net, without making sure she knew exactly how far away the ground was and how high she'd bounce once she hit it.

Today, she was taking a wild leap, and she had no idea how far she'd fall or what the bottom would feel like when she got there. Well, she imagined it might feel like Flynn's lips and the warmth of his embrace. Safe. Secure.

Today, Flynn was her parachute. She didn't know the exact specifications for how he operated or when he would catch her, but she was confident that he *would* catch her.

"Here goes nothing," she whispered.

She stood and went into the bathroom to freshen up, reapplying her lipstick while she ignored the little voice in her head that told her she was being ridiculously girly. This was her adventure, and she was going to do whatever the hell she wanted. And right now, she wanted her lips to look perfect and shiny and plum-colored when Flynn saw her in a few minutes.

She shoved her lipstick into her purse, lifted the handle to the suitcase, and left her room. There were other wedding guests in the hallway, milling about as they prepared to leave the estate. She found Megan and Jake in the parlor, talking to one of Theo's uncles.

"Morning, Ruby," Megan called, waving her over. They'd seen each other briefly at breakfast, but everyone had been so busy recounting the highlights of the wedding and talking about Elle and Theo's upcoming honeymoon in Tahiti that they hadn't had much of a chance to chat.

"Hey." Ruby rolled her suitcase over to them.

"So, you're spending the day with Flynn?"

She nodded. "I am, and I'm looking forward to it. You guys have fun on your own and stop worrying about me."

"I'm not worried," Megan said with a laugh. "Well, maybe a little."

"Don't be." Ruby gave her a squeeze. "Text me later, okay?"

"You know I will. Have fun," Megan said.

"I'll keep her from bugging the hell out of you all day," Jake said, giving his girlfriend a good-natured nudge.

"Thanks," Ruby told him. "Besides, you guys can just follow my hashtag if you want to keep tabs on me."

"Oh, I plan to," Megan said, holding up her phone for emphasis.

"Talk to you later." Ruby waved goodbye and rolled her suitcase toward the front door. The spinning, churning sensation in her stomach intensified.

Leaping without a net.

It was slightly terrifying, but once she committed to something, she was determined to see it through, and today was no different. Worst case, she and Flynn didn't enjoy each other's company as much in the light of day and would spend a boring day together. But she didn't think that was going to be the case.

As she walked outside into the gray September morning and caught sight of Flynn leaning against the side of a sleek black sports car, she knew boring would be the last way she'd ever describe the day to come.

"Good morning," he said, opening the passenger door for her. He had on jeans and a blue polo shirt that looked like a million bucks on him, his brown hair neatly combed, although a stray lock tumbled rebelliously onto his forehead. "Ready to have an adventure?"

"So ready." She let him take her suitcase before sliding into the passenger seat. The inside of the car smelled like leather and Flynn, whatever scent it was that she associated with him.

He stowed her suitcase in the trunk and climbed into the driver's seat. "Would you like to see a bit of the English countryside on our way into London this morning?"

"Yeah, that sounds great." See? She was going with the flow, embracing the adventure.

Flynn started the car, telling her random facts about the

sights they passed. He took her past rolling fields full of sheep and crumbling stone structures that looked like they'd come right out of a history book. They stopped at a castle built during the fourteenth century and took a quick tour. Ruby didn't even try to contain her glee as she read over the plaques detailing the history of the structure.

"We're standing where real knights once rode into battle. Look, you can see where a cannonball hit the wall." The stone walls of the castle were pockmarked with scars from ancient battles. She posed for several photos, posting them to the hashtag she would be using to document her adventure, #RubyGoesRogue. She even let Flynn take a silly selfie of them together in front of the entrance.

"Something to remember our day together by," he said as he texted it to her.

She looked at it as they got back into his car. They were both smiling, leaned in close. Flynn's arm was thrown casually over her shoulder. They looked good together, not that it mattered. Some of the happiest couples she knew didn't look outwardly like they'd be a good match, super girly Megan with cowboy Jake, for example.

Flynn chatted easily the rest of the way into London. He had a knack for keeping the conversation going, while Ruby tended to be more concise with her words. She was perfectly happy to sit back and enjoy the landscape and Flynn's descriptions of what she was seeing.

"Shall I drop you off at your hotel while I park the car?" he asked as they entered London's bustling streets.

She'd gotten a quick look at the city when she arrived a few days ago, but it still impressed her. So much history. Everything seemed so grand and important. "Yeah. That would be great. I'll check in and drop off my suitcase and then we can do some sightseeing."

"Perfect." He pulled the car to the curb in front of the rather ornate-looking front entrance of the Hilton where she'd booked herself a room.

"I'll meet you in the lobby in a little bit," he said. "Just come down whenever you're ready."

"Okay. Thank you." She climbed out of the car as Flynn came around to help her with her suitcase, and the concierge met them to take her bag. She said goodbye to Flynn and walked inside, pausing for a moment to take in the grandeur of the lobby.

It just looked so...British. Everything around her had a feeling of old-world opulence, thick brocades on the floors and intricately carved moldings around edges and doorways. She approached the counter and soon was on her way to her room on the seventh floor, riding up in the elevator with the bellhop who had taken her suitcase.

She tipped him and let herself into her room, exhaling deeply as she sat on the bed. This was her first time traveling alone, and it was equal parts thrilling and terrifying. Having Flynn with her here today felt good, though. Letting him show her around didn't in any way lessen her adventure, as Megan had said, and in fact, it might add to it. Surely, she was likely to see and do things with him as her tour guide that she might have missed otherwise.

She really appreciated that he hadn't come up to the room with her. It seemed to cement her impression of him being a solid guy. It probably would have been fine if he came up, but she felt a lot more comfortable having this time to get settled on her own.

She freshened up, took a quick peek out of her window to see the view—more buildings—and headed downstairs to meet Flynn in the lobby. He sat on one of the plush chairs, phone in hand, lost in whatever he was looking at on his screen.

She stopped in front of him. "Hi."

He looked up with a smile. "Ready?"

She nodded. "Where to first? I could go for some lunch."

"You read my mind. I was thinking we could go over to Camden Market, find some food, maybe poke around in the shops a bit, if that sounds good to you?"

"Sounds great."

"Okay. Would you like to take the Tube? It's easier and quicker than driving in the city."

"I've never ridden a subway before," she told him. "Florida—where I grew up—is too low and wet to have anything underground, and Rosemont Castle is too far out in the mountains. So yes, let's take the Tube. It sounds exciting."

Flynn shook his head in amusement. "Never met anyone who found the Tube exciting, but it's an experience, all right. Let's do it."

They headed outside. The weather hadn't improved since they'd left the Langdon estate a few hours ago. Gray clouds hung heavy in the sky, threatening rain, but Ruby was beginning to suspect it was an empty threat, given that it had been this way for days now. The air was cool and moist, with just the faintest hint of drizzle, and she was glad for the lightweight jacket she'd put on over her shirt. The weather app on her phone told her that this was typical for London in the fall.

"Here we go," he commented as he led the way toward the station.

Together they walked down a set of stairs from the sidewalk that led to a station beneath the street. Ruby inhaled the damp, musty smell of the Underground. People bustled this way and that, a whole new city here beneath the city they'd left behind on the sidewalk above.

She and Flynn made their way to the ticket machine, where she purchased a visitor's pass called an Oyster card and loaded it with enough money to last her a few days. They made their way down an escalator to the platform just as a train whooshed into the station, pushing a wave of warm, stale air ahead of it.

"That's our train," Flynn told her, and they joined the stream of people boarding the car in front of them. The inside of the train was shaped almost like the tunnel it ran through, with an arched ceiling. Its walls were plastered in maps with different colored lines to indicate the various branches of the subway.

Instinctively, Ruby sat across from the map so she could study it as they rode. She might as well get familiar with it now, because she would be riding alone tomorrow. She would probably spend two or three days here in London before venturing on to someplace new. The beauty of this trip was that she had an open-ended itinerary she could customize as she went, like creating her own graph. Point A to point B to point C, and she could determine the location of each point whenever it suited her, change them if she wanted to.

The doors closed, and an automated voice told them they were on the Northern line headed toward Edgware before the train moved forward with a jolt. Ruby reached for the pole in front of her to steady herself, listening to the high-pitched whine of the train as it wound its way through the tunnel. Outside the windows, it was pitch black, but inside the train car, everything was lit in a bright electric glow.

"It's bigger than I imagined," she said, tipping her head toward the map on the wall opposite them. It was a maze of different colored lines and too many stops to count. She'd need to download a copy of it onto her phone for navigating tomorrow.

"London's a big city."

They rode mostly in silence as she soaked in the experience, watching as people got on and off as they passed through various stations beneath the city. Finally, they arrived at Camden Road, and Flynn indicated that this was where they should get off. Whereas they'd descended from a busy street filled with tall, stone-faced buildings, they came out in a much more colorful section of town. The buildings were lower here, brightly painted, with vendors set up beneath their awnings.

"I'm starving," Flynn commented. "What are you in the mood for?"

"Something…different," she told him. "Something I can't get at home."

"That shouldn't be a problem, because you can get just about any cuisine in the world right here."

"Okay." She felt overwhelmed by the possibilities.

"This market used to be a distillery," Flynn told her as they walked. "It was known for producing some of the world's finest gin, as well as being a hub for all kinds of trade, due to its location here on the canal. I'll show you the old—oh look, there's the juice stand I used to visit as a boy." He had a habit of interrupting himself, his words following whatever random train of thought his brain had taken. She found it—and him—ridiculously charming.

They ended up getting Venezuelan arepas, delicious corn wraps stuffed with savory meat and vegetables. Afterward, they bought edible cookie dough on cones and strolled along the canal as they stuffed themselves.

"I feel a little bit sick after all that," Ruby said, pressing a hand against her stomach. "But wow, it was so good."

"So, I shouldn't suggest that we go shopping right away?" Flynn winked.

"God, no." The last thing she wanted to do at the moment was to try to zip a dress over her belly full of cookie dough.

"Oh, I know just the thing," Flynn said, snapping his fingers. "Are you a Harry Potter fan?"

She cocked a brow at him. "What do you think?"

"I think you look like a woman who waited around for her letter from Hogwarts once upon a time, but I would hate to make a snap judgment."

She grinned. "You'd be right about that. So, what do you propose?"

"We can walk to King's Cross Station from here, and—"

"Take our picture on platform nine-and-three-quarters?" she interrupted.

"Precisely."

She tipped her face toward the still-gray sky and laughed. She was having so much fun she hadn't even thought about plans or spreadsheets since she'd left her hotel room. The station came into sight up ahead, and she and Flynn waited in a short line to take turns posing with the trolley cart that led to the mythical, magical platform. Then they boarded a real train and headed across town to the London Eye.

"You said you wanted to do something thrilling today," he said. "I thought this might fit the bill."

"Oh, it definitely will." She felt a tingle in the pit of her stomach as she looked at the huge Ferris wheel in front of them. The closer they got, the bigger it seemed to grow. Each capsule was enclosed in glass and held about twenty-five people, which sounded faintly claustrophobic to Ruby, but she wasn't about to pass up the chance to go for a ride and take in the view of the city. "We have one like this in Orlando, but I've never been on it."

"I imagine the views here are better," Flynn said as he led her to the ticketing area, explaining to an employee that he'd booked a reservation online. When had he done that? The woman confirmed Flynn's information, and then someone was escorting them past the line. They waited for a few minutes in a private area, while Flynn avoided her questions about what exactly was going on.

And then, they were being escorted onto one of the glistening glass capsules. Ruby had a moment of panic when she realized they had to step on while it was moving, but with Flynn's hand resting reassuringly against the small of her back, she hopped on without incident, and the door slid shut behind them. Their capsule was empty except for her and Flynn, oval-shaped and rounded at the ends, completely encased in glass.

There was a bench in the middle for sitting. Beside it, a bottle of champagne sat chilling in a bucket of ice.

"You booked us a private capsule?" Ruby pressed a hand against her mouth, spinning a full three-hundred-and-sixty degrees to take in her surroundings.

"I did. You deserve to ride in style."

She turned to Flynn, heart thumping against her ribs and cheeks hot. "This is...romantic."

"Or celebratory, if you prefer," he said with a casual shrug. "There's never a wrong time to enjoy a bottle of champagne while you're a hundred and thirty meters above London."

"This must have cost a fortune." She swallowed roughly. It was amazing and wonderful, and also...too much for two people who barely knew each other.

"I have it, and today I'd like to spend it on you," he said quietly.

Ruby pressed a palm against the glass as their capsule slid slowly along the loading area. "Tell me again what you do for a living?" Because all he'd given her before was a vague line about trying different things within the family business, and that felt suddenly, painfully inadequate. She took in the expensive press of his clothes, remembering the sleek sports car he'd driven her in that morning.

Flynn sighed, turning to stare out the glass wall behind them, although there wasn't much to see yet, as they were still at street level. "My family owns Exeter Hotels and Resorts."

"Holy shit," Ruby blurted. Exeter was a chain of high-end hotels with locations all over the world. She'd never actually stayed at one because they were well outside her budget. Flynn's family was loaded. Probably the kind of loaded she couldn't really even wrap her mind around.

"It's less impressive than it sounds," he said. "Or my role in the family business is unimpressive anyway. They have me lined up to oversee a new location being built in Dubai starting next month."

"Is that not something you want?" she asked, stepping closer to him. Something restless, almost sad had come over him since they'd started talking about his family's hotels.

"It's a very exciting opportunity," he said, not quite answering her question. "I enjoy getting to see new places. I'll be living in Dubai for the next six months or so."

"It does sound exciting," she said cautiously, because it was obviously *not* exciting, or at least not in a good way, for him. But she didn't know him well enough to pry or to understand what else was at play here.

He moved restlessly around the capsule, pausing to lift their bottle of champagne. "Shall we crack this open? We've got about forty-five minutes in here to drink it."

"Well, I do like a good challenge," she said with a grin. "Let's do it."

He wrapped a cloth napkin around the neck of the bottle and popped the cork, then poured two glasses. He handed one to her, and they clinked their glasses together.

"To exciting adventures," he said.

"For both of us," she added. "Whatever or wherever they end up taking us."

"I'll drink to that."

She lifted the glass to her lips and took a sip. The cold, frothy liquid seemed to sparkle on her tongue, as heady and bright as the week ahead promised to be. She was in a private capsule on the London Eye with a handsome, chivalrous hotel heir, drinking champagne. If the rest of her week was half as exciting, she'd call her adventure a win.

They stood together in silence for a few minutes, sipping their champagne and watching London unfurl beneath them as their capsule crept toward the top of the Ferris wheel.

"Oh, I see Big Ben," she said, looking down at the over-sized clock tower that contained the famous bell. The buildings spread out below them, a mixture of sleek, modern designs and old stone structures that were works of art all on their own. In between them, the river Thames twisted like a glistening serpent, moving steadily toward the ocean beyond.

"And right over there is Westminster Abbey." Flynn pointed out the famous building.

Laid out beneath them like a postcard were all the famous London landmarks that she'd heard about and never seen. She set down her empty champagne flute and pressed her fingers against the glass. "Kind of dizzying, isn't it?"

"A little bit."

The pit of her stomach tingled as she looked at the city below, a combination of the height and the champagne. It was oddly disorienting, being alone in this little bubble suspended above the city—just her and Flynn—but also intoxicating, like she was separated from the real world, responsibilities, her past, her future. None of it seemed relevant as she glided toward the top of the London Eye. "I think I could stay in here forever."

"You'd miss fresh air." Flynn walked up behind her.

"True." It was kind of stuffy in here.

"It's nice to be suspended in time for a little while, though, isn't it?" There was something nostalgic in his tone.

"Yes." She pulled out her phone and snapped a photo of the view before asking Flynn to take one of her. She posted them both to her hashtag before putting her phone away. Ruby was going rogue right now, all right.

He refilled their glasses as Ruby looked down at the capsule below them, then up at the top, drawing ever closer. Her stomach lurched as they swooped upward. It was a ghost sensation, though, more a product of her anticipation than reality, because the capsule moved slowly enough to allow passengers to keep walking around, observing the sights without losing their footing. That dip in her stomach was one hundred percent in her own head.

She walked to the other side, taking a drink of champagne

as she went. Already, she could feel the warmth of it spreading through her body, fizzing in her veins.

"Now, isn't this better than sharing the capsule with dozens of other people?" Flynn said from behind her, his accent exaggerated either by the alcohol or her own semi-buzzed state.

"Much better."

He topped off her glass, and they drank as their capsule crested the top of the wheel. "I'm not much of a tourist here in my own city, but even I have to admit this is pretty nice."

"Hard to imagine anything topping this."

"Oh, I don't know about that," Flynn said with a smile.

She polished off another glass of champagne, by now feeling delightfully buzzed as they glided around the Ferris wheel. She set her glass down and turned, her hands landing on Flynn's chest. Before she could second-guess herself, she brought her lips to his.

He let out a rough sound at the contact, his hands settling on her waist. Their lips moved together, exploring, touching. He ran his tongue over the seam of her lips, and she opened to him. He tasted sweet like champagne and cookie dough as their tongues danced together.

Ruby felt lightheaded. The movement of their capsule combined with the champagne and desire barreling through her veins had her spinning in the best possible way. She felt like she could float right off the floor, like she might fly away, tethered to reality only by the hot press of Flynn's mouth against hers.

His fingers stroked up and down her jeans, leaving a warm trail over her hips that melted her all the way to her core, which ached with need.

"Whoa," she murmured as her fingers clenched in the soft cotton of his shirt.

"Mm." Flynn kissed his way down her jaw to her neck, nipping lightly at a tender spot below her ear that made goose bumps rise all over her body. The view was slightly disorienting as she tipped her head to the side, London laid out below them while Flynn placed hot, open-mouthed kisses over her chest. His hands swept up to palm her breasts through her T-shirt. "Perfect," he whispered.

She pressed her body against his, seeking contact with any bit of him she could touch. Her breasts pressed against his chest as her thighs met his, hips unconsciously arching forward. Flynn gripped her butt, bringing their lips back together. They kissed, and they kissed, and they kissed, until she was gasping for breath, flushed from head to foot, and feeling more alive than she could remember feeling in years.

She was so caught up in their kiss that she didn't even notice their ride was coming to an end until the capsule slid into the loading area and the doors whooshed open. She lifted her head, blinking, panting, grinning like a fool. "That was quite a ride."

4

lynn took Ruby's hand as they stepped onto the platform. Her cheeks were flushed, lips pink and swollen, glasses slightly askew, and the sight was almost enough to bring him to his knees. Ruby's fingers gripped his, her eyes going wide as she leaned against him. "Whoa. Haven't gotten my land-legs back."

"Dizzy?" he asked, resting a hand on her waist to steady her.

"Kind of feels like we're still moving."

He knew the feeling. His world was spinning too, although more from that kiss than the champagne or the London Eye. "Are you all right?"

Her head bobbed. "Yep. Just a little wobbly. Let's walk it off."

"Okay," he agreed, keeping her hand in his as they left the platform, headed for the street beyond. A little exercise would be good for both of them. His head sure as hell needed clearing.

"So, what next?" Ruby asked, looking up at him.

They strolled through the crowd meandering toward the river. "Ready to go shopping?"

"Oh." She seemed to think about this for a moment, pressing a hand against her stomach. "Yeah, I don't feel like I'm bursting with cookie dough anymore."

"All right, then. Let's go."

Thirty minutes later, he led her through the front door of one of the high-end shops on Oxford Street. He'd heard his sisters rave about this one and hoped Ruby would have a similar reaction. Her eyes widened behind her glasses as they stepped inside.

"I'm not sure I can afford anything in here, Flynn," she whispered, stopping just inside the door. Her lips twisted into a frown.

"My treat," he told her. "I insist."

Her frown deepened. "I can't let you do that, especially after you just paid for that private capsule on the Eye. I mean, we hardly know each other."

"I'd really like to buy you a dress, Ruby," he said, hoping he sounded as sincere as he felt. Sometimes, his family legacy and the money that came with it felt like a burden. But when he found something he wanted to spend it on, it felt good. "I'd like to buy you anything you want in here."

Ruby's eyes scanned the store, taking in the racks of clothing and the salesclerk already eyeing them, ready to be of assistance. She looked down at her hands and drew in a deep breath. She was going to politely bow out and leave rather than let him pay.

He swallowed his disappointment. But pride was important, and if this made her uncomfortable, then he'd take her somewhere else with more affordable clothes. The purpose of the day was for her to have fun, after all.

To his surprise, she squared her shoulders and took a step into the store. "You know what? I never splurge on myself, and I never would have set foot inside this place without you bringing me here. I came on this trip to push myself outside of my comfort zone, so let's do this."

Warmth spread through his chest, settling somewhere in the vicinity of his heart. It had been so long since he'd spent time with anyone as lovely as Ruby. Everything about her was so pure. Not innocent or naïve, just…genuine. Enchanting. He envied her ability to leap past her inhibitions. It was a shame they'd only have this one day together. "Excellent."

She glanced over at him with a smirk. "I'm going to pay for it myself, though."

"Ruby—"

"No, don't," she interrupted. "When I said I couldn't afford anything in here, what I really meant is that I don't usually consider clothes worth splurging on. I guess you could say I'm practical. Frugal, even. It probably won't shock you to find out I keep a spreadsheet that budgets my spending for each month. But I've got money set aside for this trip, and a little bit of it is going toward buying myself something extravagant."

"Only if you're sure this is what you want," he said. "We can go somewhere more affordable, or you can easily wear something you already have."

"I'm sure," she told him firmly. "I want to do this."

"All right, then." He wouldn't argue the point if it was this important to her. "So, what do you have in mind?"

"I have no idea," she told him with a small smile. "I'm terrible at this. The last time I had to pick out a dress, I let Elle choose for me. And then I put up a fuss when she wanted me to get the more colorful, extravagant dress because I'd found a simple black one that was just fine."

"Nothing black, then."

"Agreed." And then she marched across the store with her chin held high, approaching the salesclerk who'd been watching them.

"Something to wear to the theater," the clerk said with an approving nod. "Oh yes, you've come to the right place."

Ruby tossed a silly smile over her shoulder at him. She followed the clerk along a rack of dresses, letting her fingers trail lightly over the various fabrics and textures. "This one is pretty," she murmured, fingering a yellow dress.

"Oh, I agree," the clerk said, plucking it from the rack.

Ten minutes later, they had picked out a handful of dresses for Ruby to try on. He saw a rainbow of colors on the rack. Nothing black. *Good job, Ruby.*

"Will you come with me?" she asked him shyly. "You can help me pick."

"I'd be honored," he told her.

The clerk led them toward the dressing rooms. There was a sitting area with several plush armchairs and full-length mirrors along the back wall, arranged at various angles. Flynn settled himself into the nearest chair.

"May I offer you something to drink before you get started?" the salesclerk asked. "Wine? Tea? Champagne? Water?"

Ruby's eyes widened behind her glasses. "Um, water would be great. Thank you."

"And for you, sir?" she asked Flynn.

"I'll take water as well. Thank you."

She nodded and walked to a serving station along the far wall, opening a mini fridge and removing two bottles of water. "I'll get your dresses arranged for you in the fitting room," she told Ruby as she handed out the waters.

"Thank you," Ruby said, peering over at Flynn again with an excited smile.

He returned it, hoping to help encourage her and put her at ease, but she seemed to have fully embraced this new leg of her adventure. She went into the dressing room, and a moment later the clerk left, closing the door behind her.

"I'll leave you two to it," she told Flynn. "I'll be just over there. Please let me know if you need any assistance."

"We will," he told her. "Thank you."

And so, he sat there, trying not to imagine what was happening on the other side of the fitting room door. After a few minutes, the door opened, and Ruby stood there in a red dress. It hung just past her knees, sleek and form-fitting. It had a black lace overlay with flower-shaped cutouts that allowed the red fabric beneath to peek through.

He opened his mouth, but nothing came out. Embarrassed, he cleared his throat. "It's stunning."

"It's pretty, right?" she asked, walking to the full-length mirrors along the back wall. "I really like this one."

He rose and followed her, stopping a step or two behind. "I think it's absolutely perfect. I want to see you in them all, but I can't imagine anything topping this one."

She twirled in front of the mirror, drawing his attention to the way the dress flared at the knee. She ran her hands over the bodice, surveying herself critically in the mirror. "Okay, I like it, but let's keep going."

He nodded his agreement, returning to the chair as she disappeared into the fitting room. A few minutes later, she was back in a royal blue dress the clerk had selected for her. "I already tried on the yellow one," she told him. "It was too tight. I couldn't even zip it."

"Want me to ask the clerk to look for one in a larger size?"

"No, that's all right. I didn't like it as much as the red one anyway. But what do you think of this one?"

He dragged his gaze down the length of the blue dress. The fabric shimmered beneath the lighting in the store. It had a snug bodice and a full skirt that fell to her ankles. "It's beautiful."

"But?" she prompted, frowning at herself in the mirror.

"Who said there was a but?"

"I heard it in your voice. Or maybe I wanted to hear it, because I don't know why, but I just don't love it."

"That's the only reason you need," he told her. "But I happen to agree. It doesn't suit you as well as the red one. I think it's a bit too formal."

"Okay," she said with a succinct nod. "Moving on."

In the end, they didn't like the pink dress either. And so, they left the store hand-in-hand with the red dress neatly packaged inside the shopping bag that now dangled from Ruby's arm.

"You know, I'm going to need new shoes too," she told him as they set off down the street.

"Then let's go get you some."

~

Ruby lay flat on the bed in her hotel room, idling twirling a lock of hair between her fingers. She didn't want to be presumptuous here, but she just might be having the best day ever. She'd walked through a castle that dated back to the Middle Ages, drank champagne in a private capsule on the London Eye, made out with Flynn with an intensity she wasn't sure she'd felt since high school, and gone on the most extravagant shopping spree of her life.

And the day wasn't over yet.

He was picking her up for dinner in half an hour, which meant she should really get up and start getting ready. But maybe she had just another minute to lay here on her bed, feeling giddy about her day. She closed her eyes and let out a happy sigh.

Flynn Bowen of Exeter hotels. What an enigma he was. He was sweet and charming and genuinely fun to be around. He hadn't complained a single time while she shopped, had even seemed to enjoy himself. There was something sad lurking behind his easygoing veneer, though. Not a tragic kind of sad, or at least she didn't think so. More like unhappiness with his work and his role within the family business. It must be hard, having a legacy like that that you had to fulfill. What if his dreams were calling him in a different direction?

Well, it really wasn't her business, after all. He was taking her to dinner and the theater tonight, but tomorrow she'd be on her own. She needed to get on with the solo part of her adventure, even if she was already a little bit sad about saying goodbye, which was ridiculous since she'd only met him yesterday. She and Flynn had just clicked from the moment they met.

With a sigh, she sat up and walked to the closet where she'd hung her new dress. It was pretty, fancy but not so fancy that she wouldn't get other opportunities to wear it, other nights out on the town. Dates, maybe. It was time for her to go on more of those.

She laid it on the bed and stripped out of her clothes, taking a moment to freshen herself up before she got dressed. She took a wet face cloth to wipe the residue of the city off herself, rubbing her favorite lotion into her skin in its place. It smelled like honeysuckle blossoms, and the scent was familiar and soothing, reminding her of home. Not home in the sense that she'd grown up smelling honeysuckle, but she always wore this lotion. It was familiar, maybe the most familiar thing about her day so far.

She stepped carefully into the dress and zipped it up, smoothing her hands over it as she surveyed herself in the mirror. The dress had a high neckline, so it wouldn't need a necklace, but the gold cuff bracelet she'd worn to Elle's wedding should go nicely with it. She redid her hair and touched up her makeup before fastening the black strappy heels she'd bought earlier. Her toes, already painted a bright cherry red, accented her outfit perfectly.

She got the black clutch she'd used at the wedding and added her phone, credit card, and other essentials. And then—because this was her adventure and she was committed to being spontaneous—she tucked one of the condoms from the pack she'd bought in the gift shop earlier into her purse...just in case.

Finally ready, she headed down to the lobby, where Flynn waited, leaning against a column and looking at something on his phone. She paused for a moment to admire the sight of him, tall and lean in a charcoal-gray suit with a burgundy tie. His dark hair was again neatly combed, although that one unruly lock had broken free to tumble over his forehead. She'd noticed him swiping irritably at it during the day, but she loved the way it looked, the hint of carefree boyishness it added to his otherwise polished appearance.

"Hi," she said.

He looked up, his gaze traveling appreciatively from her face to her toes. "Beautiful."

She stepped forward, close enough to catch a familiar hint of his aftershave. And then, she kissed him, a quick press of her lips against his, just enough to feel the jolt of electricity that sparked in her belly every time they touched. "You look pretty handsome yourself."

"Do I?" Flynn's gaze dropped to her lips before he dipped his head and kissed her back. "I think it might just be a byproduct of standing beside you."

"Stop it." She swatted playfully at his arm. "Um, you have a little…" She reached up to wipe her lipstick off his lips.

"Ready?" he asked.

She nodded, taking the elbow he'd extended for her and walking together out the hotel's revolving door onto the street.

"I used a car service tonight, so we didn't have to concern ourselves with parking or trains whilst dressed like this." He gestured toward a sleek black sedan parked a few spots away.

"Oh." *Right.* She was going out with a hotel heir tonight. "Okay."

"You don't mind, do you?"

"Not a bit." Tonight—and this week—she was committed to rolling with the unexpected, and finding out she had a driver for the evening was definitely not a bad thing.

He opened the car door for her, and she stepped inside. London was a different creature at night, sidewalks bustling with people, glittering lights gleaming off puddles from the rain that had fallen while she was in her hotel room. The sky overhead was a murky purple as the glow of the city bled into the clouds.

They drove about ten minutes through the wet, glistening streets while Ruby admired the buildings they passed. They'd obviously entered the theater district, because she saw brightly lit marquees announcing tonight's showings. Some were classic productions with titles she recognized, others were a mystery to her. Several marquees announced stars she knew from movies and TV.

"I had no idea some of these people even acted in plays," she commented.

"You'd be surprised how many actors like to try their hand on stage."

The car pulled to the curb in front of a stone-fronted restaurant with large windows overlooking the street. Inside, strands of multicolored lights crisscrossed the ceiling, illuminating the tables below in a colorful glow. Vividly decorated tapestries hung from the walls. "I love it already," she told Flynn as they stepped out of the car.

"I thought it would suit you." He led the way inside.

Jazz music played softly as the hostess brought them to a small table along the back wall, below a huge painting of a man and a woman making out. She sat, allowing her gaze to wander around the restaurant, absorbing the ambience. Everything was funky, colorful, and eclectic, exactly her aesthetic.

"I'm impressed," she told Flynn.

"By the restaurant?"

She fixed her gaze on his. "That you thought it would suit me."

He leaned forward slightly, the reflection of the overhead lighting dancing in his eyes. "Was I right?"

"Yes." She grinned at him. "If the food is half as good as the décor, it'll be a definite win."

"The food is excellent," he told her.

"Have you eaten here before?" Because although this place

suited Ruby, she couldn't quite picture Flynn bringing one of his undoubtedly high-class girlfriends here.

"The truth?"

"Of course."

He leaned back in his chair. "My sister and her wife own this restaurant."

Ruby sat up straighter. "Oh. Then I guess you have eaten here before."

"Too many times to count. And I wouldn't have brought you to my sister's restaurant if I hadn't been so sure you'd love it. I don't want to make tonight about meeting my family, although Pippa and Amy are sure to pop by at some point."

"Pippa is your sister?"

He nodded. "She's the second youngest in the family."

"Second to you," she said, remembering that he was the youngest of five.

"That's right."

Their waitress, a young, energetic-looking woman with purple streaks in her blonde hair, approached their table with a wide smile. "Oy, Flynn, I didn't know you were coming tonight."

"It was a last-minute decision," he told her.

"I'm Marlie," she told Ruby.

"Hi, Marlie. I'm Ruby."

"Nice to meet you, Ruby. Any friend of Flynn's is a friend of ours. American, hm?"

Ruby nodded. "I'm in town for a friend's wedding."

"Theo Langdon's wedding?" Marlie asked, eyes widening. "The whole city's been buzzing about it. I heard it was quite the to-do."

"Yes. Elle's one of my best friends," Ruby told her.

"Too cool. Can I get you guys started with something to drink? A bottle of wine?"

Flynn gave Ruby a questioning look. "Wine?"

"Yes, definitely."

They selected a bottle of Cabernet Sauvignon, and Marlie left them. Ruby and Flynn studied their menus in silence for a minute, the rhythm of their conversation having been interrupted.

"So, I was under the impression all your siblings worked for the family business," she said finally.

"The rest of us do. Pippa had a bit of a falling out with my parents a while back."

"Because she's gay?" Ruby asked quietly, hoping she wasn't prying into things that were none of her business.

Flynn nodded. "That was certainly part of it, although Pippa was always more taken with the restaurant industry than hotels, truth be told."

"Have they reconciled, Pippa and your parents?"

"For the most part. My parents can be a bit old-fashioned sometimes." Flynn's expression was pained. "It's not an excuse. There's no excuse."

"I'm sorry," Ruby murmured. "I don't mean to pry."

"You're not. I'm the one who brought you to my sister's restaurant on essentially our first date." He winked at her.

"It's just…" She couldn't not tell him, not when it was such an important part of who she was, but it was a conversation that hadn't always gone over well with her dates in the past. "I've been in Pippa's shoes, although luckily my parents were much more supportive."

Flynn's brows drew together. "You're…?"

"Bisexual," she told him. "Most of the time, especially lately, I date men, but I had a long-term girlfriend in college. We were together for two years."

"I had no idea," Flynn said, still looking somewhat shell-shocked, but whatever she saw on his face, it wasn't anything unpleasant. "Thank you for telling me."

"I hope it doesn't bother you." She'd gotten mixed reactions from men she'd dated in the past, everything from awkward-ness to inquiries about a threesome, but women had often been just as uncomfortable. Sometimes, Ruby felt caught in a weird in-between place with her sexuality.

"It doesn't bother me in the slightest." He reached out to grip her hand where it rested on the table. "If anything, it adds to your intrigue, and I don't mean that in a weird 'lesbian fantasy' kind of way. I just…I really like you. You're different from most women I meet, a little bit quirky and just one-hundred-percent comfortable being yourself."

Ruby opened her mouth and closed it again. She took a sip of water from the glass in front of her. "Well, thanks, I think. I wish I saw myself as confidently as you do."

"You don't?" he asked, looking genuinely surprised.

"You're seeing a different side of me here in London," she told him. "Usually, I'm the predictable, nerdy girl with the laptop and the spreadsheets, remember?"

"You keep telling me so, but I don't think I could ever find you boring." He leaned forward, grinning conspiratorially. "And I happen to find nerdy incredibly sexy."

"Do you?" She hardly recognized her own voice, it sounded so breathless…so *flirty*.

"Absolutely." He stroked his thumb back and forth over the palm of her hand. "But I think I find everything about you sexy."

"Now you're just flattering me." And she was helplessly smitten with this man she'd spent only one day with.

"Perhaps," he admitted. "But it's also true."

"I'm a gamer," she told him, going for broke. "Pretty much the extent of my social life is meeting up with my local online gaming group to play together."

"Still sexy," he told her.

She lifted her eyebrows. "Seriously?"

"I don't know anything about video games, but now I want to."

She grinned. Could he possibly be any more charming? She never wanted this night to end.

A woman with dark hair wearing a long Bohemian-style skirt approached their table with arms extended, leaning in to kiss Flynn on each cheek. "I couldn't believe it when Marlie told me you were here tonight."

Flynn gave her an affectionate hug before turning to Ruby. "Ruby, this is my sister, Pippa."

5

---

*F*lynn watched as Ruby and Pippa chatted like old friends. Maybe he'd known they would hit it off. Maybe it was part of the reason he'd brought Ruby here tonight.

"What show are you guys going to see?" Pippa asked.

"*Wicked*," Ruby told her. "I've had the soundtrack in my playlist for years, and I've always been a huge fan of *The Wizard of Oz*. I can't wait to see it in person."

"Oh, you're going to love it," Pippa told her. "Amy and I saw it last year."

"It's my first show, so I can't imagine it will disappoint."

"Your first?" Pippa asked, eyebrows raised.

"Yeah. I'm from Florida. We have a lot of theme parks, not so much theater," Ruby said.

"Well then, you're in for a treat, and I'm sure my brother is just the person to show you around London."

"We've had a blast today." Ruby looked over at him, her expression full of a pure kind of affection that made his chest feel too tight.

"I'll leave you two to your meal, but I hope you have a

wonderful time tonight, and if you ever find yourself in London again, please do stop in."

"I definitely will," Ruby told her.

Pippa leaned in to give him another hug. "I love her," she whispered in his ear.

He nudged her away playfully. "See you later, Pippa."

Pippa waved over her shoulder as she walked away, only to be replaced by Marlie, who brought their bottle of wine and took their dinner order.

"Alone at last," Ruby said with a wink as Marlie headed toward the kitchen.

"Perhaps I didn't think through the logistics of bringing you here," he admitted.

"Do you bring dates here often?" Ruby asked, sipping her wine and watching him closely.

"You may be the first, come to think of it."

"Interesting." She took another sip. "Well, for the record, I really like your sister. I'm glad you brought me here."

"You haven't tasted the food yet," he teased, attempting to downplay the unexpectedly intimate moment.

"I'm sure I'll love it, but even if I don't, I've enjoyed the rest of the experience enough to make up for it."

"I'm glad."

Conversation flowed easily as they drank their wine, although he was distracted by the way the overhead lights played in Ruby's hair. She wore it up again tonight—he was beginning to think she hadn't been exaggerating when she told him she always wore it that way—but it shone with reflected red and blue and green tones, shifting like a kaleidoscope as she moved her head.

He could stare at her all night, or it felt like that, anyway. He'd never had much luck keeping his focus on any one person or task, a byproduct of his ADHD. But right here, right now, he felt like Ruby could hold his attention forever.

"What are you thinking about?" she asked.

"I just…I've really enjoyed today."

"Me too." She smiled, eyes crinkling behind her glasses.

Their meals arrived, and they fell back into easy conversation as they ate. Ruby spun each bite of pasta around her fork, twirling it round and round before popping it in her mouth. How was it possible for every single thing about her to be so lovely and captivating and sexy?

"So, what's involved in overseeing a new hotel location being built?" she asked between bites. "Is it a project management kind of job, or are you involved with the building itself?"

"A little of both," he told her. "My background is in architecture, although as I'm sure you can imagine, the hotel has strict brand standards to follow."

"Architecture." Her eyes met his. "Is that what you enjoy most, then?"

The question he'd been asking himself for years now. "Perhaps. When I'm between assignments at Exeter, I sometimes take on side projects. In fact, I'm about to design a new house for a friend of mine. I'll be driving out to visit the property tomorrow."

"That sounds exciting."

"I'm looking forward to it," he told her as he cut a bite of steak.

"I bet," she said. "It sounds like you get a lot more creative input on your side projects than you do at Exeter."

"Yes. That's what I enjoy most about them."

"Then I'm glad you get the chance to do both."

After their meals had been cleared away, he took her hand as they walked outside. "We can walk to the theater from here, if you're up for it."

"Yes, definitely. I could use a little fresh air and exercise after that meal." She patted her belly. "Before we sit down for a show."

"I feel the same way."

They strolled down the street together, dodging puddles

here and there. The air had cooled now that night had fallen. Ruby rubbed her hands up and down her arms, and he silently cursed himself for not suggesting she get a jacket or wrap to go with that dress. It was much warmer in the southern United States than it was here in London, so it probably hadn't occurred to her that she might need another layer.

"Here." He shrugged out of his jacket and wrapped it around her shoulders.

"Thanks." She hugged it around herself gratefully. "You're not cold now, are you?"

"Not at all."

It was only a few blocks to the theater, and soon they were making their way to their seats. Ruby had given back his jacket when they went inside, and consequently, he found himself admiring the way her dress shimmered beneath the low lighting of the theater as she walked.

"Wow," she whispered as she turned to take in her surroundings. "It is so ridiculously gorgeous in here."

The theater had been built in the eighteenth century and was decked out in classic grandeur, with ornately carved wood and red velvet seats. He'd been here before, but looking at it through Ruby's eyes helped him to remember how splendid it truly was. Perhaps he ought to take a page from her book and seek this kind of pleasure in his everyday life.

"Do you mind?" Ruby took out her phone, gesturing for him to lean in for a selfie. They posed together for several photos with the stage behind them. She'd been photo-documenting their day, sharing the photos on a hashtag she'd started so her friends and family could keep up with her vacation.

"Would you like me to take one of you?"

"Sure." She posed against the railing, one leg crossed over the other, with the stage behind her and a radiant smile on her face. He was tempted to ask her to send it to him to remember tonight by, but it was probably better he didn't. A clean break would make it easier for him to move on with the next chapter of his life in Dubai.

Ruby spent the next few minutes flipping through the playbook, familiarizing herself with the cast and the theater. And then, the lights dimmed.

∼

RUBY WAS STILL SMILING AS THEY LEFT THE THEATER THREE hours later. "That was amazing."

"Maybe you should see another show while you're in town," Flynn suggested.

"I just might." She hooked her arm through his as they walked out onto the street. "I booked my hotel room for three nights. I could do this again tomorrow and the next night if I wanted to."

"Will you fly home at the end of your three nights in London?"

"No, I've got another week until my flight home. I was thinking about seeing more of Europe, but I'm not sure where else I could go without adding another flight, which could get complicated…and pricey."

"Scotland is very nice," Flynn said. "You could also take the EuroStar to Paris."

"What's the EuroStar?"

"It's a high-speed train that runs under the English Channel. It'll take you from London to Paris in about two and a half hours."

She stopped in her tracks, looking up at him. "I had no idea that existed, and I've always wanted to visit Paris. I might totally do that."

"You should." He gave her hand a squeeze. "I think you'd enjoy it."

"I think I would too," she agreed, ideas unfurling inside her brain like one of the tapestries in Pippa's restaurant. She could visit the Louvre, climb the Eiffel Tower, sit at a sidewalk café while she sipped wine and ate amazing cheese and pastries. Already, she couldn't imagine doing anything else to finish out her adventure.

"Are you up for one more stop tonight?" he asked. "There's someplace I'd like to show you."

"Sure." She ought to be exhausted, but she was too high on the excitement of the day to feel it. "Where are we going?"

"It's right around the corner," he told her.

"Okay," she agreed easily. He hadn't steered her wrong yet, and she wasn't quite ready for their day together to end. They rounded the corner together, and Flynn guided her toward the entrance of a fancy hotel, tucked back from the street and grand in the way of many buildings here in London, like it was etched in history. The word Savoy was illuminated over the entrance, and it sounded vaguely familiar, although she wasn't sure where she'd heard it before.

"The Savoy is probably the most famous hotel in London," Flynn told her. "And it has one of the most famous bars as well. I thought we could stop in for a nightcap before I take you back to your hotel."

A concierge in a black suit with white gloves held the door open for them as they walked inside. The lobby looked like it had been carved out of marble, glossy and important, its floor a patchwork of black and white squares like a chess board. She paused just inside the door, taking it all in, before following Flynn as he strode across the room like he owned the place. Briefly, she wondered if he did.

Then they were being escorted into another room, a lounge dotted with luxurious-looking leather seats and framed black-and-white photos on the walls. There was a piano near the rear of the room, at which a man in a black suit sat playing soft jazz music. Flynn gestured for Ruby to sit in a curved over-large seat meant for two. She slid onto one end of it, and he sat beside her.

"This is called the American Bar," he told her as he passed her the drink menu. "And I didn't bring you here because you're American." A smile touched his lips.

"No?"

"It's a well-known spot here in London. A place to see and be seen, if you will. I thought it might be a nice addition to your adventure."

Ruby darted a quick glance around the room. It was the type of place she'd never come on her own, fancy and expensive and exclusive. And it felt like the perfect place to wrap up this day. "It's perfect."

They ordered drinks while Flynn explained some of the history of the hotel and the bar to her. The black-and-white photos on the wall were all celebrity portraits, as glamorous as the room itself. As it turned out, the drink menu was inspired by the portraits. The cocktail she chose, called "The Debut," was inspired by a photo of mother and daughter actresses Judy Garland and Liza Minelli, shot to celebrate Liza's debut in showbiz.

Ruby thought it seemed fitting tonight, as she debuted this new side of herself. She sipped from her drink, feeling sophisticated and worldly in this posh bar with a handsome man at her side. If she squinted her eyes, softened her focus just a bit, she thought any one of the glamorous stars from the photos around them might walk into the room, brought to life in startling color.

"Penny for your thoughts," Flynn said, sipping his own drink.

She grinned at him. "I'm just thinking how fancy I feel right now."

"You look very fancy as well," he told her, his gaze dropping to her dress.

Heat spread over her skin in its wake. Good God, she'd had a lot to drink today, between their champagne on the London Eye, wine with dinner, and now this. It was a lot more than she usually drank, but it had been spread out enough that she'd never gone beyond comfortably buzzed. Now though, she felt her inhibitions slipping away.

"Do you come to places like this often?" she asked.

"Truthfully?" His gaze locked on hers. "No."

"Really?" That did surprise her. He had the money and class to do this every night.

"I actually prefer to leave the hotel world behind when I'm not working," he said with an amused sort of smile that didn't quite reach his eyes.

"What do you enjoy, then?"

"That's the million-dollar question, isn't it?"

She'd touched that nerve again. "You don't enjoy your job."

He looked away, taking a long sip of his whiskey. "I enjoy many things. I just seem to have trouble making any of them stick."

"Do you have to work for Exeter? I mean, couldn't you do your own thing like Pippa?"

"I could." He didn't elaborate, so she decided not to pry.

"Well, I'm a good listener if you want to talk about it," she said. "And I'm a safe person to talk to, since you never have to see me again after tonight."

"A shame about that last part," he said, before his expression softened. "And I appreciate your offer. It's nothing nearly that serious. I just haven't found my place within the company yet, that's all."

"I'm sure you'll find it soon."

"Thank you."

They shifted to safer topics as they finished up their drinks. Flynn called for his driver to pick them up, and then they were in the car, headed for her hotel. Ruby felt a bit blurred around the edges, a mixture of alcohol and emotion. Their day together had come to an end, but she wasn't ready for it to be over. If she was fully committed to embracing her wild side on this trip, then she had to own the part of herself that unabashedly wanted Flynn in her bed tonight.

"I'll walk you in," he said when they arrived. He walked into the lobby with her, pausing to kiss her, a soft, gentle kiss that nonetheless lit every cell inside her on fire.

"Would you like to come up?" she asked, emboldened by the events of the day.

"Are you sure it's what you want?" he asked, ever the gentleman, even as his pupils dilated with lust.

"Positive." She hooked her fingers in the lapel of his jacket, fitting herself up against him.

"I don't want to do anything you'll regret in the morning."

She lifted her chin to whisper in his ear. "The only thing I might regret is letting you walk out that door right now."

A slow, sexy grin spread across his face. "All right, then."

His next kiss was nothing like the first. This was a kiss with intention, a promise of the pleasure to come. She ran her fingers down his tie, feeling his warmth, his strength as her knuckles grazed the front of his shirt. And then she led the way toward the elevator.

6
———

*R*uby swiped the keycard and led the way into her room. She flicked on the small light by the door, which threw a soft glow over the rest of the room, casting deep shadows everywhere. On the far side of the bed, London glittered outside the window.

She looked at Flynn, momentarily tongue-tied as she took in the sight of him in her hotel room. He looked so handsome in that charcoal-gray suit, so posh, but at the same time, just Flynn, the man who'd been charming her since the moment they met. It might seem impulsive, inviting him up to her room, but she was doing this for herself, taking what she wanted for once, no holding back.

"Seems impossible we've only known each other for twenty-four hours." She stepped closer, tugging at the knot of his tie, loosening it before tossing it over the chair behind him.

"It does." He settled his hands on her hips, toying with the lace shapes cut into the design of the dress.

"Do you do this a lot?" She wasn't sure why she'd asked, because she didn't really care what the answer was. She already knew everything she needed to know about him for tonight's purposes.

"What do you think?" he asked, his gaze never wavering from hers.

She unfastened his belt and pulled it free. "Probably more often than I do."

"Maybe, but that's still not very often." He brought his hands up to cup her face, pressing his lips to hers. His kiss was as intense as it was brief, leaving her gasping for breath as he lifted his head. "It sounds like tonight is out of the ordinary for both of us."

"I like that," she whispered, shivering with pleasure as his hands slid over her shoulders and down her back, leaving a trail of heat in their wake. He gripped her ass, bringing her hips against his.

"I can't even begin to tell you how sexy I find you in this dress." His voice sounded like he'd swallowed sand, thick and gritty. "Which is not to say I haven't found you sexy in everything I've seen you in, because I have. But this dress..." His fingers bunched in the lace overlay, tugging gently.

"That's a shame."

"Why?"

"Because I'm ready to take it off."

Then they were kissing again, mouths meeting messily as their hands roamed, groping for buttons and zippers. She had his shirt halfway unbuttoned by the time he'd unzipped her dress. But instead of removing it, his hands went to her hair, gently removing the clasp that held it in a knot on the back of her head. It tumbled down her back, settling against her exposed skin, and Flynn groaned in appreciation.

"That's better."

It'll only get in the way while we're having sex, she started to say but stopped herself. If he wanted to see her with her hair down tonight, she was happy to indulge him. She took off his jacket and pushed his shirt over his shoulders, revealing the undershirt beneath. "So many layers," she teased as she hooked her fingers beneath the hem and lifted it. He raised his arms, allowing her to slide it over his head.

"More like it." She ran her fingers over his bare chest, appreciating his athletic frame and the coarse rub of his chest hair beneath her fingertips.

"My turn." He slid the dress down her arms, helping her to step out of it. He tossed it on the chair behind them, his gaze raking appreciatively over her body. "And you, by comparison, have very few layers."

She'd foregone a bra tonight since the dress had a fitted bodice, and as a result, she was now standing before him in nothing but black satin panties while he still had on his pants. She reached for him, intending to level the playing field, but he was kissing her again as his hand slid down her stomach. He stroked her over her underwear, and the hum of desire that had been buzzing through her veins elevated to a roar.

"Yes," she gasped, her hips moving to the rhythm of his fingers, her senses overwhelmed by the throbbing need he'd ignited in her core.

"You're so beautiful, Ruby."

She fumbled the button on his pants, finally freeing it and pushing down his zipper. Flynn stepped out of them, tossing them in the direction of his shirt and her dress. His boxer briefs tented impressively in front, and she ran her palm over his length, thrilled with the feel of him, so hard. It had been over a year since she'd had sex, maybe two, and she felt absolutely starved for his touch, to feel him on top of her, inside her, literally everywhere.

"Hurry," she mumbled, pushing his briefs to the floor before stepping out of her panties. She lay back on the bed, drawing him down with her.

"What's this?" He slid down to press his lips against the little red bird tattooed on her hip.

"I got it after my bone marrow transplant, once I was well."

She gasped as his tongue swirled over her skin, hot and wet. "To celebrate being able to spread my wings."

"You were free of your cage," he murmured against her hip, his breath sending goose bumps over her skin.

"Yes." She curled her fingers into his hair, wanting to keep him there, but also wanting to feel him everywhere.

"I'd say you've flown pretty far." He kissed his way over her belly to her breast.

"I didn't at first," she said, her voice gone whisper-soft with pleasure. "But I am this week."

He took her nipple between his teeth, tongue flicking against the sensitive nub, and she made a sound she didn't even know she was capable of as desire rolled in a hot wave through her body.

"Oh my God," she panted.

"You like that?" He looked up at her with a smug smile before turning his attention to her other breast.

"Mm hmm." She arched her back, increasing the pressure of his mouth. Her legs slid against his, their hips rocking together in an imitation of the act their bodies were demanding. His cock pressed against her, and the ache between her thighs grew. "There are condoms in the table beside the bed."

Flynn lifted his head, eyebrows raised. "You came prepared."

"I'm a woman of the twenty-first century," she told him. She might not have her spreadsheets this week, but that didn't mean she couldn't still plan ahead. "Besides, I bet we'd have only had one if I'd left it to you."

He gave her a rueful look. "Guilty as charged, and grateful for this modern woman who will allow us to properly enjoy our night together."

"As you should be." She nipped at his earlobe, giving him a gentle nudge toward the side of the bed.

He opened the drawer and grabbed a condom, leaving the box on the table for easy access before covering himself.

"You're a woman of many surprises, Ruby Keller," he murmured as he settled himself over her.

"I'm trying, anyway."

He reached between them and stroked her, circling her clit, and she groaned, tilting her hips into his hand, seeking more pressure, more friction, more everything. He withdrew his fingers and replaced them with his cock, pushing into her in one long, slow stroke.

"Fuck, yes." He withdrew and thrust again, stretching her, filling her.

"Yes," she echoed, swamped in sensation. She drew him closer, feeling the weight of him against her, the rough scratch of his chest hair against her sensitive nipples, the incredible heat building between them as he pounded into her. That unruly lock of hair bounced over his forehead with each stroke, adding something endearing to the otherwise erotic image of him hovering over her, eyes blown with desire, sweat beading on his brow as he grew closer to his release.

They rolled to the side, and her hair twisted around her neck, choking her. She pushed at it, raising up on one elbow to free herself while Flynn chuckled. He swept it back, settling her against the sheets as they resumed their previous rhythm.

"Flynn," she said, but it sounded almost like a whine. She clawed at him, trying to bring him closer, arching her back to increase the friction where their bodies met.

"I've got you, love," he murmured, bringing a hand between them. He rubbed her clit, matching the rhythm of his hips as he pounded into her, and she sighed in relief even as the desire inside her coiled impossibly tight, ready to burst.

"Yes," she moaned. "Just like that."

Flynn made a sound of agreement, stroking harder, faster. Her feet left the bed, wrapping around his legs as her eyes closed and her breath caught.

"Oh God," she gasped, and then she was coming, release

rolling through her like a wave that left her weak and tingly in its wake.

Flynn dropped his head to kiss her, his movements becoming more frantic, hips bucking against hers until he broke with a groan, his hips going still, his cock pulsing inside her as he came. Neither of them moved, arms wrapped tight around each other, panting for air, giddy grins on their faces.

She reached up and tugged at that lock of hair hanging over his forehead. "Stay the night?"

~

FLYNN WOKE IN STAGES, FIRST AWARE OF THE WHISPER OF RUBY'S breath in his ear, the tickle of her hair over his chest, the vaguely sweet, feminine scent of her. He'd always loved the way women smelled, but Ruby was especially lovely. Everything about her was lovely. In another time, under other circumstances...

But he was incredibly thankful for the day they'd shared.

Beside him, she stirred, peeking over at him out of bleary eyes. "Morning."

"Good morning." His voice was scratchy, rough with sleep.

"Do you have to go already?" she asked, snuggling closer. She looked different first thing in the morning, bare faced without her glasses, hair spread out across the pillow behind her.

He was already infatuated with her, but this vision of "first thing in the morning Ruby" was definitely going on his list of favorite things he'd ever seen. "Not quite yet," he told her.

"Good." She leaned in and kissed him. First thing in the morning Ruby wasn't as sweet and innocent as she looked, though, because before he knew it, she'd rolled on top of him, and their good morning kiss had turned into something a lot hotter.

They kissed and teased, hips rocking as the city came alive

outside the hotel window. Her hair hung like a curtain between them, getting in his face and tangling beneath his arms, causing more laughs as she lunged for a hair tie on the nightstand and pulled it back. By the time he rolled on a condom and pushed inside her, he was wishing like hell he didn't have to say goodbye. They moved together in the soft morning light, their gasping breaths and moans the only sound in the room.

Ruby came first, throwing her head back as she rode him right over the edge. He gripped her hips, thrusting up into her until he'd joined her in release.

"Hell of a way to say goodbye," she said with an impish smile.

He pulled her down against his chest. "Wish it didn't have to be goodbye."

She dropped a kiss against his neck, snuggling against him. "So do I."

They lay like that for several long minutes as they caught their breath and their bodies cooled. He tugged the band out of her hair, tracing shapes through its shiny depths.

"I'm meeting my friend Megan and her boyfriend Jake for breakfast this morning before they fly home," she said finally, looking up at him. "Would you like to join us?"

"I'd like that," he said.

"Me too." She gave him a quick kiss before sitting up. "I need a shower before we head out."

They spent the next half hour or so getting ready. He put on his trousers and button-down shirt from last night, but left off the tie and jacket he'd worn to the theater. Ruby dressed in form-fitting black jeans and a multi-colored top that billowed over her chest and clung to her hips. She dried her hair and clipped it up in her usual style, applying minimal makeup that emphasized her natural beauty.

"So, what's on your agenda for the day?" he asked as they left her room, trying to keep the wistfulness out of his tone.

"I have no idea," she said with a twinkle in her eye. "It's all part of the adventure."

"Will you text me?" He cleared his throat, feeling suddenly awkward. "I mean, if you feel like it. I'd love to see where your journey takes you."

"You can follow me on social media," she told him as they waited for the lift. "It's hashtag Ruby Goes Rogue."

"I'll do that." With a ding, the door to the lift slid open, and they stepped inside.

Ruby leaned in, pressing her lips against his ear. "But I might text you anyway."

They walked outside into the cool, gray London morning, with Ruby leading the way toward the café where they would meet Megan and Jake.

"Does the sun ever come out here?" she asked, squinting up at the sky, which was fairly bright despite the overcast haze in the air.

"It does, although fall is our rainiest season, so this is likely to be the kind of weather you see for the majority of your trip, I'm sorry to say."

"It's okay," she said. "I don't really mind it. Mother Nature can't rain on my parade."

"That's the spirit."

They walked several blocks before she turned left, following GPS directions on her phone. She stopped in front of a glass-fronted café. "This is the place."

A woman inside—Megan, presumably—waved excitedly when she caught sight of them. Ruby waved back, clasping Flynn's fingers in her own as she led the way inside.

"Hi," the brunette said with a wide smile. "I'm Megan, and this is Jake." She gestured to the man beside her, who nodded politely.

"Flynn Bowen. Very nice to meet you."

"Likewise," Megan said, still smiling. "We've all been dying to meet the man who swept Ruby off her feet the other night."

"Megan." There was a slight rebuke in Ruby's voice, but she was smiling too. "He didn't sweep me off my feet so much as untangle me from a rosebush."

"This is very true," Flynn agreed.

"Ah, you guys are adorable." Megan gestured to the empty seats at the table. "Sit down. We waited for you to order."

Flynn and Ruby sat across from her friends, exchanging casual conversation until the waitress approached to take their breakfast orders.

"Coffee?" Ruby asked in disbelief when the waitress walked away. "I thought you guys only drank tea."

"I hate to break it to you, but we Brits drink almost as much coffee as you Americans do, although I do enjoy a good cup of tea." This morning, he needed the extra caffeine boost of coffee after being up half the night with Ruby, working their way through that box of condoms, but he thought it best not to mention that detail in front of her friends.

"Flynn, what do you do for a living?" Megan asked.

"My family owns the Exeter line of hotels and resorts," he told her. "I'll be overseeing the newest location in Dubai beginning next month."

Megan's eyes widened dramatically. "Um, wow. Sorry. Just...ouch!" She glared at Ruby, who had obviously kicked her under the table.

"Don't mind her," Jake said amiably. "She's nosy and easily flustered."

"I am neither of those things," she said, giving him a look of mock exasperation before returning her gaze to Flynn. "Sorry for being dramatic. I know Theo has a lot of rich and important friends. I just didn't realize I was having breakfast with one of them."

"Wishing you'd held out for one of Theo's rich friends?" Jake asked, eyebrows raised.

Megan's expression softened as she gazed adoringly at him. "Hardly." She nudged him playfully with her shoulder. "It's funny. Of the three of us—Elle, Ruby, and me—I probably would have been most likely to say I wanted to fall in love with an earl or a hotel heir. But I would have been wrong, because I only have eyes for the horse trainer." And she turned and kissed Jake full on the mouth.

Ruby cleared her throat. "Get a room, you two. Anyway, Flynn and I aren't together, really. Not after this morning, anyway. He's got to get back to work, and I'm carrying on with my solo trip."

"Maybe your solo trip needs to keep you here in London a bit longer," Megan stage-whispered to Ruby with a wink.

Ruby mock-glared at her. "Solo trips are, by design, meant to be undertaken alone."

An air of awkwardness descended over the table then. Megan turned to say something to Jake, and Ruby gave Flynn an apologetic glance before fiddling with the contents of her purse. Their food arrived soon after, and they turned to more casual topics again as they ate. Megan and Jake were headed straight to the airport after breakfast.

"I've already been away from the horses longer than I'm comfortable with," Jake explained. "Not that I don't trust the guy I've got looking after them, and I've sure as hell enjoyed our trip to London, but it's time to go home."

"And one of us needs to get back to the castle," Megan said. "We run an inn out of Rosemont Castle," she explained to Flynn. "We closed it for the long weekend since we were all here for Elle and Theo's wedding, but we've got guests booked tomorrow night."

"It's finally your turn to run the inn on your own," Ruby told her with a teasing look. "I bet you'll be calling before the end of the day with questions."

"I will not." Megan pointed a fork in her direction. "Just because you and Elle have handled most of the business end of things up until now doesn't mean I can't do it."

"I'm just ribbing you," Ruby said. "Call anytime you want. I'll be missing you by then anyway."

Flynn watched, fascinated by the easy rapport between them. He was glad to know Ruby had Megan—and Elle too—in her life back home. He knew what it was like to have that kind of bond. He shared it with Pippa to a greater degree than his other siblings, but also with Aidan, who'd been his best mate since childhood and who Flynn would be working with for the next few weeks as he designed Aidan's new home.

They finished their meal, and Megan and Jake said their goodbyes. She and Ruby hugged before they headed out, leaving him and Ruby alone at the entrance to the café.

"I guess this is where we part ways too," he said.

"I suppose it is." Ruby went up on her toes and kissed him, not a quick peck on the lips, but a deep, delicious kiss that reminded him of all the reasons he wished he didn't have to let her go. Finally, she stepped back, her smile tinged with the same nostalgia he was feeling. "Thanks for these last two days. It's been amazing."

"It really has."

"I don't think I've ever had this kind of connection with someone I just met before." Her hands were still clasped in his. "And I really would like to keep in touch. I mean, at least a few messages here and there to let each other know what we're up to. That's not weird, is it?"

"I think it would be weirder if we didn't, don't you?" He squeezed her fingers. "I would genuinely like to hear about the rest of your trip, and to keep in touch after that, even if we have to limit our relationship to being friends."

"That's what I was hoping for too. Well, I guess we'd better just get this over with, then." She leaned in and gave him another kiss. "Goodbye, Flynn."

"Goodbye, Ruby." He drew her in against him, holding her close for a long moment, and then he let her go, walking briskly down the street to hail a taxi.

7

Ruby stood in the entrance to the café, sucking in deep breaths that did little to calm the jittery feeling that had overtaken her. Her heart raced, and her palms had gone damp where they clutched her satchel. Yesterday had been magical, exactly the kind of adventure she'd dreamed of. Now, she was really and truly alone in London, alone in a huge, bustling city an ocean away from home. And she was absolutely terrified.

Before she knew what she was doing, her feet were already carrying her toward her hotel. She speed-walked the whole way there, halfway winded by the time she made it to her room. She put the Do Not Disturb sign on the door and turned the deadbolt before flinging herself face down on the bed, coughing as she caught her breath. The sheets were a rumpled mess, and they smelled like a mixture of sex and Flynn.

She'd thought yesterday was the first day of her solo adventure, thought Flynn—being little more than a stranger—was part of that adventure, but now she realized he'd been a crutch. He'd led the way yesterday, guiding her, keeping her on track. Now, she had to do what she'd intended to do from the start and create her own journey.

At that moment, she would have given anything for the comfort of her laptop, to bury herself behind its screen and come up with a detailed itinerary for the rest of her day. But that was exactly why she hadn't brought it. She was supposed to take this week to teach herself how to fly blind and appreciate the moment.

Carpe fucking diem, Ruby.

She grumbled at herself, thumping her fists against the mattress. She'd been on her own for all of fifteen minutes, and she'd already locked herself in her hotel room and thrown a pity party for one. Of course, she could make an itinerary on her phone, but *not* doing it was the whole point.

She sat up and glanced around the room. Her red dress was still tossed over the chair from last night. The whole room was a mess, really, and she'd never been able to tolerate a mess. That was one thing she could fix. Resolutely, she got up and hung her dress in the closet before straightening up the rest of her things. Then she got her satchel off the desk and put her e-reader, a bottle of water, and a granola bar into it. She freshened up in the bathroom and unbolted the door.

Look out world, because Ruby's solo adventure had just begun.

Outside, she paused on the sidewalk, wondering where to go. Truthfully, she was exhausted, and the damp weather had given her a bit of a cough. She and Flynn had been nonstop yesterday and then up half the night. Today seemed to call for a quieter approach. She remembered him mentioning a park with views of the city, and that sounded like exactly what she needed this morning. Google suggested Hampstead Heath might be what she was looking for, so she set out.

She walked to the Underground station and stood there, staring at the huge map in front of her. So many colors. So many different lines. An overwhelming maze of trains to choose from. Truthfully, she had no experience riding public transportation. She could spend hours analyzing a transit system of this size, figuring out the best routes to get herself everywhere she wanted to go.

Since that was out of the question, she consulted her phone to find the closest subway stop to Hampstead Heath. She swiped her card without difficulty and rode the escalator down to the platform. A train was already sitting in the station, and she ran to catch it, wedging herself in with the crowd and trying not to step on anyone's toes. She'd ridden four stops before she realized she was going the wrong way.

Frustrated, she got off at the next station and boarded a train headed in the opposite direction. Almost an hour later, she exited at Kentish Town, so flustered by her subway ride that it took her several long minutes to get her bearings and locate Hampstead Heath. On her way into the park, she stopped to buy a small blanket. She walked aimlessly for a little while, enjoying the scenery. Eventually, she climbed Parliament Hill and spread her blanket over an open patch of grass. She sat, legs extended before her, and took in the view of the city below.

Now, this was more like it. She reached into her satchel and pulled out her phone, snapping a quick photo of her surroundings to share on social media.

Totes jealous! came the text from Megan. *We're about to board.*

Have a safe flight, Ruby responded. She got out her e-reader and lay back to read. The sky overhead was still heavy and gray, the air cool but not uncomfortably so. Hopefully, it didn't start pouring while she was out here. She made it through a chapter of her book, but soon the words began to blur before her eyes, and she shut them, just for a moment to rest.

The next thing she knew, a shriek startled her awake. Her eyes blinked open, focusing on a group of teenagers nearby, playing a raucous game of soccer. She rolled onto her belly, fumbling for her phone to see how long she'd been asleep, and holy crap, it was past noon already. She'd slept away the whole morning.

Irritation prickled in her chest, because surely she ought to be doing something more productive with her day than sleeping in a London park. But no, she was not going to feel guilty about this. Her reasons for being tired this morning were exciting and adventurous, and anyway, this was her trip to do whatever she wanted, no judgment from anyone else, including herself. Obviously, she'd needed the sleep.

She sat up, stretching as she glanced around to make sure she still had her satchel. She *would* be pissed at herself if someone robbed her while she slept, but everything was still here. Her skin felt cool and damp from the London weather, but at least she hadn't gotten rained on. Her stomach was clamoring for lunch, and she had to pee, so she packed up her things. She crammed the blanket into her satchel and headed for the exit, deciding to walk until she came across someplace that looked good for lunch.

As she walked, she scrolled through the notifications on her phone, pausing as she found a text from Flynn. *Nice view! How's your day going?*

He'd obviously found the photo she'd shared earlier while she was sitting up on Parliament Hill. A warm tingle spread through her belly.

Moving at a slower pace today, she texted with a winking emoji. *But no less fun.*

That was a lie. Yesterday had been one of the most amazingly fun days of her life, but Flynn didn't need to know she was struggling to find her balance today, that she was fighting an underlying sense of panic about not knowing where she was headed next. Yesterday, he'd kept her moving, so busy and enamored with his company, she hadn't even realized she'd been flying without a net. Today, it was all she noticed.

Glad to hear it, he replied.

She shoved her phone into her bag as she walked through the gates leading out of Hampstead Heath. After looking both ways, she headed left, which looked like the direction with more restaurants. Twenty minutes later, she was comfortably nestled at a table in the back of a little sushi restaurant with a plate of tuna maki in front of her.

This was a start, but she still couldn't shake the nagging sense of unease, the urge to bullet point the rest of her day. She had a lot of work to do to truly achieve her goals for this trip.

~

It had taken Flynn most of the morning to drive to Aidan's new home site in Wales. After stopping for lunch, they'd spent several hours surveying the property together. Flynn was completely taken with the location, nestled into a wooded hillside that overlooked the Wye River Valley. Peaceful. Invigorating. He could already picture a house here, built with local wood, rustic but with a sleek, modern look, big windows and a deck overlooking the valley.

"I love that," Aidan said, nodding excitedly as Flynn explained his vision. "Can we put a hot tub on that deck too, mate?"

"Of course." Flynn laid out the surveyor's map on a rock between them and spent the next hour determining which would be the best location for the house and how to orient it. Energy flooded his system as things began to fall into place. His vision combined with Aidan's to create an idea that truly excited him. This house would be something unique that reflected his friend's needs and allowed Flynn to challenge himself in ways he hadn't been able to at Exeter.

He walked the property, snapping photos on his phone as he noted the specific angle and coordinates to capture the best views. Before putting his phone back into his bag, he thumbed quickly through his notifications, somewhat disappointed not to have a new text from Ruby. She was enjoying her vacation the way she'd meant to now…on her own.

"You have a new girlfriend you haven't told me about?"

Aidan asked, sitting sideways in the front seat of his car, feet in the dirt, watching as Flynn worked.

"No." Flynn pushed his phone into his pocket and returned to his measurements.

"Someone you're keen on, then?"

Flynn ignored him and continued with his work.

"You've been checking your phone all afternoon like a man who's waiting to hear from a woman he fancies," Aidan continued. "So, who is she?"

Flynn sighed, walking over to lean against the side of Aidan's car. "Her name is Ruby Keller. I met her at Theo's wedding. We spent the day together yesterday in London. But that's all. She's on with the rest of her vacation now."

"And you're wishing you were still with her."

"Maybe a little," he admitted. "We had a really nice time together. It's a shame the circumstances are what they are."

"And what are they, exactly?" Aidan asked.

"She's American. She actually works at Rosemont Castle, helps manage the property for Theo."

"Interesting," Aidan said, scuffing his heels idly through the dirt.

"And I'll be heading to Dubai at the end of the month to oversee the new Exeter hotel being built there."

"That does pose quite a logistical problem," Aidan agreed. "What do you say we continue this conversation down at the pub? Have you gotten everything you need?"

"For today," Flynn said. "I'll need to come back out here over the next few days while I'm drafting up your plans."

"So, the pub, then?"

"Yes, all right." Flynn packed up his materials and walked around to the passenger side of the car. "Truly exceptional spot you've got here, Aidan. It's going to be a hell of a property."

"I'm sure it will be now that you've signed on to design it for me. You've got real talent, mate. You're wasting it building hotels that all look exactly like the next."

"Well, it's my job to build hotels." He slung his briefcase into the back and sat in the passenger seat beside Aidan.

"I appreciate you taking on this project for me," Aidan said as he backed the car out of the wooded lot toward the road. "I know you're busy right now."

"My pleasure. This is a nice change of pace for me."

They chatted as they drove into town and parked in the little public lot behind the main street. As they waited for the hostess to seat them, Flynn checked #RubyGoesRogue and saw a new photo, a selfie she'd taken outside Buckingham Palace, grinning widely, still wearing the multi-colored top she'd had on when he kissed her goodbye that morning. Heat spread through his gut, coiling into an uncomfortable mixture of longing and regret.

"Is that her?" Aidan asked.

"Yeah."

"She's still in London, then?"

Flynn nodded. "For one more day, I think."

"And why aren't you there with her?"

"Because I'm here with you," Flynn told him pointedly. He'd lost focus and gotten sloppy on the job enough times, but he'd never shirked work for a woman. "And also because she already had a trip planned before she met me."

"That's a shame."

Flynn looked again at the photo of Ruby. She was beaming, smiling so widely her eyes scrunched into slits, the way he'd seen her do yesterday as they explored the city together. She was having fun, embracing her solo adventure the way she'd intended. So, he swallowed over the pang in his chest and put the phone away. "It's for the best, really."

RUBY WRAPPED UP IN THE HOTEL'S FLUFFY WHITE ROBE AND TOLD herself she wasn't hiding. It was perfectly acceptable to order room service for dinner and watch cheesy movies in bed on her second night in London. So what if last night this time, she'd been sitting with Flynn at the theater, watching her first West End play?

It felt like hiding, though. She sighed as she took another bite out of her burger and flipped through channels on the TV. She encountered BBC after BBC after BBC, but none of the shows she scrolled past appealed to her.

Today wasn't a failure. If she repeated it in her head enough times, maybe she'd start to believe it. She'd had breakfast with friends, spent the morning at the park (sleeping, but still...), had a lovely lunch on her own, and visited Buckingham Palace. Since she hadn't planned ahead, she'd missed the changing of the guard, and the public tours had been sold out for the day. But she'd still gotten to see the palace from the outside.

She'd had fun. She really had. But the whole day, in the back of her mind, she'd had this lingering sense of panic, feeling out of control, lost. Maybe it had been a mistake to try to take an unplanned trip. Why hadn't she just created a detailed itinerary before she left Virginia? That way she could truly enjoy herself.

It wasn't that she minded being alone. Sometimes, she preferred being on her own. But right now, she missed her laptop so much she could cry. Some people needed lists and order to function, and she was one of them. Why had she thought it was so important to push herself out of her comfort zone?

With another sigh, she carried her now-empty room service tray out to the hall and shut and bolted the door with the Do Not Disturb sign out. While Ruby had been hiding behind her laptop, Elle and Megan had both followed their passions, started new businesses, and fallen in love. Not that this trip was part of any plan to fall in love, because if meeting Flynn had taught her anything, it was that meeting the right person at the wrong time might be worse than not meeting them at all.

But—and she would never admit this to anyone, not even

her closest friends—there was a tiny, needy part of Ruby's heart that craved the kind of fairytale romance Elle and Megan had found. She wanted to be swept off her feet by a Prince—or Princess—Charming and live happily ever after. Hopefully, this trip was either the first step in breaking herself out of her shell or a last solo jaunt before she fell in love. Or maybe both.

Speaking of Elle, a text message from her popped up on Ruby's phone. She clicked on it, bringing up a smiling selfie of Elle and Theo against a backdrop of turquoise water.

Loving Tahiti. May never come home. jk. Miss you guys already!

Megan had already replied with a string of emojis, and Ruby was hit with a wave of homesickness so strong it physically hurt. She missed her friends so much...

Have a fruity drink for me! she typed and pressed SEND.

Then, she curled up in bed with her e-reader. A few hours later, because she was still tired after last night, she decided to turn in early. Tomorrow was a new day, and it would be a better one.

That mantra was still fresh in her mind as she got up and got ready the next morning. She again packed her satchel with water, snacks, and her e-reader...just in case. Then, she headed out in search of breakfast. Lured by the scent of coffee and scones, she ended up eating at the restaurant in her hotel.

"...the Elgin Marbles," a woman at the table behind her said. "I've heard they're simply stunning in person."

Ruby's interest peaked. She'd heard of the Elgin Marbles, a collection of classic Greek sculptures, and maybe she'd had a vague idea that they were at a museum here in London. A quick Google search led her to The British Museum, which sounded fascinating. The freaking Rosetta Stone was there! She'd always been taken with museums, but truly spectacular history and art weren't easy to come by in Orlando, Florida, where she'd grown up. Here in London, though...

Decision made, she finished her breakfast and left the hotel.

Today, she was confident as she swiped her Oyster card and rode the subway across town.

Seven hours later, she was exhausted but exhilarated as she left The National Gallery, having museum-hopped all day long. She sank onto a bench in Trafalgar Square, watching as children ran in shrieking circles around the statue-filled fountain at its center. She released a happy sigh, her brain stuffed comfortably full of all the amazing things she'd seen today. She'd posted an obscene number of photos to her hashtag, wanting to document it all. And now, she swiveled in her seat and took a selfie with the fountain behind her.

Today, her smile wasn't fake. This time, she was smiling from the inside out. She was having a great time and had embraced the freedom to move from one museum to the next whenever it pleased her, no schedule to break.

How to finish off her last day in London? She closed her eyes and let her mind wander. What did she want to do tonight? A fancy dinner on her own? Maybe dancing in a posh club? No, that wasn't really her style, and the last thing she wanted tonight was to be hit on by random guys in a bar.

Another show. The thought crystallized in her brain, and she smiled. Yes, she wanted to go to the theater tonight, and she knew just what she wanted to see, if she could get a last-minute ticket. She'd noticed the other night that *Hamilton* was playing here, and she had been dying to see it for years.

She unlocked her phone and downloaded a ticketing app, checking tonight's schedule. There was a showing at eight, and as luck would have it, there was a single seat in the upper balcony still available. Ruby's heart gave a little leap as she completed her purchase. Showtime was only two hours away.

She stood and headed with purpose toward the Underground entrance at the other side of the plaza, coughing as she walked. It was a dry cough, though, and she felt fine. She was taking plenty of extra vitamins and supplements to boost her immune system for this trip. Probably, she was just allergic to something in the London air.

She rode home, stopping at the market near her hotel for a quick dinner. Back in her room, she eyed the red dress in her closet. She'd only worn it for a few hours the other night, and no one who'd seen her that night would be seeing her tonight.

Decision made, she stripped out of her clothes and slipped into it. As she surveyed herself in the mirror, a myriad of memories blew through her. She saw herself at dinner with Flynn in Pippa's funky, amazing restaurant, holding his hand in the theater as they watched *Wicked*, sipping overpriced but delicious drinks together at the American Bar in the Savoy Hotel.

"Tonight, I'll make some new memories in this dress," she told herself, turning her attention to her hair and makeup. This would always be her London dress.

She put a few essentials in her black clutch and headed out. Since she didn't want to ride the subway dressed like this, she let the concierge hail a taxi for her. It was a short ride to the theater, and she felt a flutter of excitement as she stepped inside, allowing herself to be swept up in the tide of patrons bustling toward their seats. She bought a glass of wine and a program before making her way to the balcony.

She busied herself with her program until the show started, sipping from her wine and feeling very sophisticated here in this glamorous theater, about to enjoy what was sure to be an amazing performance. Hoping it didn't lessen her coolness, she spun in her seat to snap a selfie with her wineglass and the stage visible behind her.

Hamilton was everything she'd hoped it would be…and then some. She laughed. She cried. And she rode back to her hotel with a big, silly grin on her face. She'd had a wonderful day today, all by herself and completely agenda-free. This was her last night in London, or at least the last night she had booked at her current hotel.

Flynn had mentioned a train to Paris, and she knew without thinking that's what she was going to do. Tomorrow morning, she'd check out and go to Paris. She could find and book a hotel while she was on the train. Then, she'd spend the last three days of her trip soaking up as much of France as she could.

That tingle of excitement in her belly was back. This was the adventure she'd come to London hoping to find.

She swiped her keycard in the door and stepped inside her hotel room, again bolting it with the Do Not Disturb sign out. But tonight, she wasn't hiding. Tonight, she was basking in the victory of a successful day. She wasn't tired, though. On the contrary, her blood coursed through her veins, swift and hot, vibrant, alive.

She caught sight of herself in the mirror and paused. *This dress.* She ran her hands over the front of it, remembering the way Flynn had touched her two nights ago, the way he'd gripped her hips, the way their bodies had pressed together. A warm ache grew between her thighs, and she squeezed them together.

She slid the zipper down her back, remembering how Flynn had paused after unzipping it to take her hair down before removing the dress. She did the same thing now, letting her hair fall down her back, tickling the exposed skin there. She stepped out of the dress and hung it in the closet. She'd pack in the morning because right now, she was…distracted.

Maybe horny was a better word for it.

Wearing just her panties, she went to her suitcase and searched through the zipper pouch that contained all the odds and ends she'd brought that didn't belong in her toiletry bag. Nail polish, vitamins, her back-up glasses in their case, and a little cloth pouch at the bottom that contained her vibrator.

This was her make-it-up-as-she-went adventure, after all. And right now, she wanted an orgasm. She stepped out of her panties and tossed them into the pile of dirty clothes at one end of her suitcase before crawling onto her bed. The sheets were cool against her bare skin, drawing an involuntary gasp from her lips as she lay back. She slid one hand between her legs, picturing the way Flynn had looked here in bed with her, the way his eyes gleamed almost black when he was aroused, the scrape of his chest hair against her breasts, and the feel of his cock as he pushed inside her.

With a moan, she reached for her vibrator and switched it on.

8

---

*T*hinking about you right now.

Flynn stared at the text from Ruby on his phone, as surprised as he was aroused by her words. He'd seen the photos she posted on social media today, following along virtually as she explored some of London's finer museums and then took herself to the theater. She hadn't texted him since shortly after he left London, so he'd decided it was probably best to let things end there.

But now her name was on his screen, and his heart was pounding like he'd just finished a workout at the gym.

Is that so? he replied.

Mm hmm.

Where are you? he asked, not wanting to read too much into this, but it was nearly midnight, and it was hard to picture her anywhere other than...

In bed.

Those two words and the images they conjured sent a burst of fire straight to his groin. He leaned back in the desk chair, rolling his shoulders. He'd been deep into the design for Aidan's new house when she texted, having spent an untold number of hours in his auto-CADD program laying the groundwork for his design. Now, he saved the program and exited, closing his laptop. Nothing was going to distract him from this project—not even Ruby—but it was late, and he'd made great progress today. He'd come at it again tomorrow with fresh eyes.

Then, before he could lose his nerve, he picked up his cell phone and dialed.

"Hi." Ruby sounded breathless, maybe even aroused, but it was hard to read too much into one word.

Flynn adjusted himself inside his trousers, somewhat embarrassed by the reaction he was having to the sound of her voice. "How are you? Your photos look like you had a good day."

"It was an amazing day." Her voice was soft, pitched in a way he recognized from their night together, a way that only increased the pressure in his pants.

"Ruby…" He wasn't sure what to say. Surely what he thought was happening, wasn't actually happening.

"This is such a bad idea," she whispered. "I should hang up."

"Don't hang up," he blurted. "Are you touching yourself right now?" He had to know, had to be sure he wasn't inventing some sort of sex fantasy in his head.

"No." A hint of something coy entered her tone. "But I am using my vibrator."

Jesus Christ. Flynn gripped himself through his trousers, suddenly aware of the faint buzzing sound that traveled through the line. "Describe it for me."

"It's black. Tear-shaped. Soft on the outside. It feels almost like skin when it's warm…like a cock."

"Like my cock?" He stood, fumbling with the buttons on his shirt, wanting to strip out of his clothes but too impatient to undress himself.

"Yes." Her breath hitched, and his cock was about to burst through his trousers.

He unzipped his pants and freed himself, sucking in a harsh breath as he took his aching cock into his fist.

"Are you doing this with me?" she asked breathily. "Because I'm not that interested in describing things while you just sit there and listen."

"I am." He gave himself a firm stroke. "But you've got to slow down a bit and wait for me to catch up." Because she already sounded close, *really* close.

"Flynn…" It was a whine, and he pictured her sprawled across the bed in her hotel room, one hand between her legs, the other on the phone, breasts bouncing as she panted for breath.

"Does it have levels?" he asked as he kicked off his shoes and slid onto the bed, leaning against the headboard. He left his shirt on, trousers open in the front as he stroked himself.

"Yes."

"Turn it down, then," he said, heat building low in his gut as he worked.

"Flynn." This time it sounded more like a reproach, but the buzzing got softer, and Ruby grumbled into the phone.

"Keep talking to me," he told her. "You'll help me get there faster. Tell me what you're doing."

"Cursing your name is what I'm doing," she said with a little whimper that made his cock surge beneath his fingers.

"Tease yourself for a few minutes." He gripped tighter, stroked harder. "For me."

"Umph." Her voice was muffled, as if she'd pressed her face into the pillow. "I turned it off. Now I'm touching myself, just enough to be ready when you are."

"That's right." His voice was a growl, his cock painfully hard beneath his touch. He could come so fast talking to her like this. But then it would be over. She'd hang up, and he might never speak to her again. "Getting close."

His balls tightened, and he stilled his fist, holding steady until the sensation had passed. A drop of pre-cum glistened at the head of his cock, and he rubbed his thumb over it, spreading it over his skin, groaning at the sensation.

"Flynn," Ruby panted in his ear. "You're killing me here."

"Almost there, love." He gave himself one long, slow stroke, almost overcome by the strength of his need, the desire to hear her come, to lose control while she whimpered and panted her release into his ear.

"Hurry." Her voice had gone high-pitched again, the way it did right before she came.

"Slow down for me, Ruby."

"You're not dragging this out on purpose, are you?"

"Maybe a little," he admitted. "I wasn't ready for it to be over yet."

"Flynn." This time, her voice was definitely a rebuke, broken by a gasp. "You want to drag this out? Fine, stop touching yourself."

He stilled his hand. "Why?"

"Just do it." She gasped, her breaths coming in rapid pants, and then a low sound of relief.

Flynn's cock throbbed so hard he thought he might come even without touching himself. He squeezed his eyes shut, listening to the sound of her orgasm, savoring the arousal curling around his spine, throbbing in his cock.

"Holy shit," she whispered, sounding relaxed now. "Okay, now it's your turn to slow down and wait for me."

"Again so soon?" he asked, ridiculously aroused by the idea of her coming again for him.

"With this thing?" The buzzing started again. "I'll be there with you in no time."

"Okay, then." If he had a few minutes to kill, he might as well get out of the rest of his clothes and get properly comfortable here in bed. "If I were there, I bet I could make you come even faster."

"I bet you could too," she said on a gasp. "You're awfully good with your hands. And your mouth."

"Wish I could come over there right now and show you." He'd gotten out of his shirt, but now he had to pause and stroke himself, unable to bear the pressure in his cock.

"Where are you?" she asked, seeming to consider the possibility.

"I'm in Wales, almost three hours from London," he told her, shoving his trousers down his legs and kicking them to the floor.

"That's a shame," she whispered. "But the combination of the vibrator and your voice is doing wonders anyway."

"Glad to hear it," he gritted as he began stroking himself in earnest. "Because I'm about to explode over here."

"Tease yourself for me, Flynn," she said, throwing his earlier words back at him.

"Getting harder to do, no pun intended." He slowed his pace, taking several deep breaths to keep himself in check.

"I'm almost there." She was panting again, and the buzzing got louder.

"Yes." He let himself go, then, his fist moving at a frenzied pace as everything inside him clenched and tightened, centered in the throbbing need in his cock. Ruby whimpered, and it was the match that lit his fuse. His balls tightened as fire licked its way down his spine, and then he was coming in hot spurts against the sheets, groaning as release flowed through him. Vaguely, he was aware of Ruby moaning her own release in his ear, and then they were both quiet, breathing heavily.

"Goddamn," he managed, his voice hoarse.

"That was one of the hottest things I've ever done," she whispered. "I'm…I'm glad you called when you did."

"Yeah, me too."

"I'm going to Paris in the morning." Her voice was soft, sleepy, satisfied. "Thanks for helping make London special for me."

"I think you did that all on your own, but I'm glad I could be a part of it."

"Goodnight, Flynn," she whispered.

"Goodnight, Ruby." He hung up the phone and lay there, sprawled across his hotel bed, too tired to move, but the ache in his chest—the one he felt every time he thought of never seeing Ruby again—felt a hundred times stronger now than it had earlier today.

~

RUBY STEPPED OFF THE EUROSTAR TRAIN JUST BEFORE NOON THE next day, eyes wide as she pulled her rolling suitcase into Paris's Gare du Nord train station. Here she was, entering her second new country in a week. She spoke a little bit of French. She'd taken classes in college, and so she'd been trying to decipher bits of conversation here and there ever since she boarded the train in London earlier that morning, although she hadn't had much success.

She'd seriously overestimated the strength of the EuroStar's WiFi signal, and consequently, she had arrived in Paris sans hotel. All the seats in the station seemed to be occupied, so she rolled her suitcase over to the wall and stood, scrolling through nearby hotels on her phone. She covered her mouth and coughed, flinching at the dull ache in her chest. She rubbed at it absently, fighting back a growing sense of panic.

Yesterday's occasional cough had become more persistent, although she'd been in denial about it as she rode on the EuroStar. Now, she was wishing she'd stayed in London, where she spoke the language, in case she ended up having to go to a clinic or hospital. With her medical history, this cough could easily become pneumonia, if it wasn't already.

And she didn't even have a hotel. She swallowed hard as she clicked on a website, desperate to get out of this loud, crowded train station. The hotel was affordable and touted itself as being near tourist destinations. It had a good customer rating, and she didn't have the time or energy to be picky. It would do.

She reserved a room and rolled her suitcase outside to join the line of people waiting for a taxi.

Once she'd made it into a cab, she showed the driver the address of her hotel and settled back in her seat, stifling another cough. The taxi slid through the streets of Paris, and Ruby stared transfixed out the window, taking in the gorgeous architecture, buildings with ornate stone facades and flower boxes in each window. As they rounded a corner, she caught a glimpse of the Eiffel Tower in the distance. Her pulse jumped, pushing back some of the fear and helplessness that had overtaken her. She was in Paris, for crying out loud. There was no way this part of her adventure wasn't going to be awesome, immunodeficiencies be damned.

The taxi pulled up in front of her hotel, a quaint-looking brick-fronted building, tall and narrow, sandwiched between its neighbors like commercial townhouses. A bright red awning over the front entrance greeted her. Maybe the color was a good omen for her upcoming stay. She thanked the taxi driver, paid, and got out, letting him help her with her suitcase.

Inside, she was relieved to discover that the front desk staff spoke English. The friendly young woman behind the desk gave her a key to a room on the fourth floor and directed Ruby toward the elevator. She rode up and let herself into her room. It was small but pretty, with a double bed in the middle and a window that overlooked the tree-lined street below. A vase of real flowers sat on the desk. She leaned in to smell them, inhaling their rich floral scent before doubling over in a coughing fit.

She sat on the bed, taking slow, shallow breaths until it had eased, wiping away the tears that had formed in the corners of her eyes. She opened her satchel, pulled out a bottle of water, and took a long drink. When she inhaled, mucous rattled in her chest. *Dammit.*

It had been over a year since she'd had so much as a cold, years since she'd been seriously ill. But, like it or not, she was sick now. She was going to have to see a doctor before this got any worse. Maybe, if she treated it early enough, she could still salvage some of her time in France.

But first, she was going to enjoy lunch in this lovely city. She spent a few minutes settling into her hotel room and then set out. She hadn't gone two blocks before she stumbled across an adorable-looking café. It even had a table available outside on the patio overlooking the street.

She ordered a salad with a side of fresh bread and leaned back in her chair, satisfied to relax and people-watch for a little while. Her phone dinged with an incoming text message.

How's the adventure going? Are you still in London? It was from Megan.

Ruby cleared her throat, swallowing past the urge to cough as she texted her back. *Just arrived in Paris.* She took a picture of the view from her table and sent it to Megan.

Super jealous! I hope you're having an amazing time.

I am, except I'm getting sick. She inserted a frowny-faced emoji. *I think I'm going to have to find a doctor this afternoon.*

Her phone immediately began to ring.

"Are you okay?" Megan asked as soon as Ruby had connected the call. "What's going on?"

"Just a cough," Ruby told her. "But I'd like to stay ahead of it if I can."

"Absolutely," Megan agreed. "I can hear it in your voice. You sound hoarse. Are you sure you want to stay? Maybe you should catch a flight home tonight."

"I'll see what the doctor says, but I'm not going to take any unnecessary risks, I promise." A part of her wanted nothing more than to book the next flight home, but she didn't want her trip to end like this, not if she could help it.

"I just wish someone was there with you," Megan said. "Promise me you'll think about coming home early?"

"I'll think about it." Ruby sipped her water. "But it's just a cough. It's probably nothing."

"Maybe." But Megan didn't sound convinced, and Ruby could hardly blame her. She'd nursed Ruby through more illnesses than she cared to admit—including several bouts of pneumonia.

"I'll keep you posted as soon as I know anything, I promise."

"Okay. So how are things otherwise? You're still having fun?"

She looked around. The street the café was on looked like something off a postcard. Here and there, she caught snatches of conversations in French. "I am, or at least I was in London. Paris has gotten off to a rocky start, but hopefully I'll be able to sneak in some sightseeing despite this cough."

"Your pictures have been so cool," Megan said. "We've all been following along with your trip on social media."

"I know." Ruby smiled as she took another sip of water. "You've been liking and commenting on my posts like crazy."

"Well, we're excited for you. Have you seen Flynn again?"

"No, but I talked to him last night." A warm tingle spread through her belly at the memory.

"You did? What did you guys talk about?"

"Nothing I can tell you while I'm sitting in public." Ruby pressed a hand to her cheek, which was flaming hot.

"Oh my God," Megan squealed into the phone. "Did you guys have phone sex?"

"Yes," she admitted with an embarrassed giggle, then covered the phone with one hand as she stifled a cough. "It was really hot."

"Why didn't he come to Paris with you?"

"I already told you, he's working, and besides, this trip is supposed to be all about me."

"Yeah, but you should hear yourself when you talk about him, Ruby. Your voice gets all dreamy. I mean, really, when's the last time you were this smitten with anyone?"

She cleared her throat and took another sip of water, pressing a hand against the ache in her chest. "It's been a while."

"Elle and Theo made a trans-Atlantic romance work. Maybe you and Flynn should try too."

"The situations are totally different. And I mean, we only spent one day together."

"Well, I still think you should come home, but if your cough were to clear up…I'm just saying, he's in Europe. You're still in Europe. Maybe try to see him again if you think this thing between you two is worth fighting for."

~

FLYNN DIDN'T MAKE IT BACK TO HIS HOTEL ROOM UNTIL PAST nine that evening. He'd spent most of the day with Aidan, running through all the particulars of his build, noting updates and adjustments that needed to be made to the rough mock-up Flynn had put together yesterday. Now, he had a mountain of work to do, but it could wait until tomorrow. Tonight, he needed to relax for a bit.

He set the carry-out bag that he'd brought home from the pub on the table, his stomach rumbling as the scent of beef and potatoes met his nose. He set out his meal, cracked open a beer, and thumbed through social media on his phone while he ate. Ruby had posted a series of photos of Paris landmarks, taken from what looked like the inside of one of those tourist buses that took people around to all the points of interest. Briefly, he wondered why she'd decided to ride the bus today, but that was secondary to the pang of regret in his chest that she'd left London.

This wasn't a surprise. He'd known she was only in London for three nights. Hell, he'd been the one to suggest the train to Paris. But it felt real now, in a way it hadn't before, that he wasn't going to see her again.

He looked over at his laptop. He'd finished surveying the site and gone over all the particulars for the house with Aidan. Technically, he could complete the design from anywhere. Of course, it would be more professional to stay here in Wales, to be able to show Aidan his progress and get his feedback along the way. But he had a feeling Aidan would be the first person to give a green light to Flynn taking a quick excursion to Paris.

Before he got ahead of himself, he'd just shoot her a text, see what she was doing tonight. He opened his text messaging app, feeling a punch of lust in his gut when he saw their most recent texts, the ones that had led to their ridiculously amazing phone sex. If she'd texted him last night from bed while she was pleasuring herself, surely it didn't violate the rules of their relationship if he texted her now just to say hello.

Bonsoir, chéri. How's Paris?

Her reply came almost immediately. *Much sunnier than London.* She added an emoji of the sun for emphasis.

Most places in the world are sunnier than London. Feel like chatting for a few minutes?

This time, there was a lengthy pause before she started to type, a pause he tried very hard not to overanalyze. It was totally fine if she didn't want to chat. For the best even, maybe.

Sure, she answered finally.

Not giving himself a chance to second guess the decision, he pressed the little icon next to her name.

"Hi." Her voice was soft, almost hushed, and the sound of it made his stomach swoop like he'd just gone over the big drop on a rollercoaster.

"I didn't wake you, did I?"

"Nope. Just relaxing in my hotel room before bed."

"Same."

A loaded silence fell over the line as he remembered what they'd done together on the phone last night. He suspected she was remembering the same thing.

"Would you like some company tomorrow?" he asked before he could lose his nerve.

There was another pause as she seemed to consider this.

"Company, as in…?" she asked, still speaking in that hushed

voice. Was there someone else in the room with her that she was trying not to disturb? No, that was ridiculous.

"As in, I could fly out to Paris for the day. I'd really like to see you again."

"I…" She paused and cleared her throat. "I'd like to see you again too, Flynn, but I'm not sure it's a good idea."

"Of course," he said quickly, fighting the sting of disappointment. "No need to complicate things when you're only in Europe for a few more days." It had been a ridiculous request, really. His parents had been disappointed time and again when he lost focus in the middle of a project, and here he was doing it to Aidan too. This had felt different, but maybe it was exactly the same.

"Yes." She sounded relieved. "I mean, I like you…a lot. But I planned this trip as a solo adventure, so I really think I need to do it on my own. And besides, it would only be harder to say goodbye a second time, don't you think?"

"I'm sure you're right."

"Sorry."

"No need to be," he told her.

"I'll always cherish our day in London," she whispered.

"So will I."

"Goodbye, Flynn."

"Bye." He set the phone down on his desk and looked at his mostly cold dinner. Last night, they'd said goodnight. Tonight, they'd said goodbye.

9

*R*uby set the phone on her nightstand and rolled over in bed, coughing. She wanted to call Flynn back, throw caution to the wind and invite him to Paris to spend another magical day together. She probably would have done it too, if she weren't sick. She'd gone to a clinic that afternoon and gotten medicine for her cough. The doctor had listened to her lungs and told her to come back tomorrow if things had gotten any worse.

And they definitely hadn't gotten any better. So, she'd probably wind up back at the clinic tomorrow, would probably leave with a pneumonia diagnosis and antibiotics, hopefully could avoid IVs and a hospital stay. Either way, a romantic day with Flynn wasn't in the cards. And besides, she meant what she'd told him. If they spent any more time together, it would only make it harder the next time they had to say goodbye.

She'd quit being resentful of her faulty immune system years ago. This was just how her body worked. But damn, the timing really sucked this time. Of course, her whirlwind trip had probably caused her to get sick in the first place. At least she'd gotten in a sightseeing tour of Paris this afternoon, in case she spent the rest of her vacation in bed.

Her phone dinged with a text message.

Feeling any better? It was from Megan.

No worse, anyway.

Megan sent a sad-faced emoji. *Come home tomorrow, please? I'm so worried about you being over there all by yourself.*

Let's see how I feel in the morning first, but I'm thinking about it.

It felt like a failure to end her trip early, to crawl home weak and sick. But, if it came to that, she'd do it. She wasn't about to fool around with her health and wind up in the hospital.

Okay, sweetie. Call me tomorrow.

I will. Promise. xx

She put her phone down and measured out another dose of the cough syrup the doctor at the clinic had given her. It burned down her esophagus, making her grimace. It was ironic, given her condition, that she'd always been terrible at taking medicine.

She walked to the window and looked out, hugging herself against the chill in the air. Below, people strolled by on the street, so leisurely compared to the way Americans walked. No one rushed. Couples walked arm-in-arm, talking and gazing at each other affectionately. An elderly woman paused to wave to someone across the street before crossing to talk to them.

Please let me feel better tomorrow so I can go out and experience the rest of Paris.

The tour bus this afternoon had been a poor substitute for exploring the city on her own, but she'd needed to rest if she hoped to kick this thing before it kicked her, so she'd opted to sit idly in climate-controlled comfort while the bus took her around the city. She'd even worn a mask to protect herself from germs.

Tomorrow will be better.

She washed up for the night and climbed into bed, taking that sentiment with her as she drifted into a deep, drugged sleep.

FLYNN SPENT A QUIET DAY AT HIS LAPTOP, WORKING ON THE blueprints for Aidan's house. He sat at the desk in his hotel room, breaking only briefly for food and to stretch his legs. By dinnertime, the design was nearly complete. The house was sleek and modern, yet rustic enough to fit seamlessly into its surroundings. It had all come together nicely, and truth be told, he was feeling pretty damn good about what he'd created.

He ordered himself a sandwich from the restaurant downstairs and turned to his phone. After avoiding it for most of the day, he finally gave in to his curiosity. He wanted to see what Ruby was up to in Paris today, even if it hurt to know he wasn't there with her. When he typed in her hashtag, though, nothing new popped up since her photos from the bus tour yesterday. That was unusual. She'd been photo-documenting every moment of her trip up until now. Why hadn't she posted pictures of her adventures today?

He frowned, as the feeling that had been nagging at the back of his subconscious since their phone call last night finally broke through. She hadn't sounded like herself. Something had felt...off. Combined with her lack of photos today, he couldn't help the frisson of worry that snaked its way through him.

They'd said goodbye last night. He'd promised himself he wouldn't contact her again. And he was going to honor that promise, just as soon as he made sure she was okay.

Missed seeing your photos today. Hope all's well! He typed the message and sent it before he could change his mind. He expected Ruby shoot back a coy response about how she'd spent the day in bed reading or at the rooftop pool, maybe that she'd decided to take a break from social media.

Instead, he was met with silence.

That didn't necessarily mean anything. At this time of night, she might be out to dinner with her phone at the bottom of her purse. Maybe she'd lost her phone. That wasn't a comforting thought, but it wasn't especially horrible, either. Ruby was a resourceful woman. She'd get herself set up with a new one in no time.

He ate his supper, took a shower, and stretched out in bed to watch some television. Still no response from Ruby. There were a million reasons for her not to reply, the most innocent of which being that she might just not want to talk to him. But he had a hard time believing she'd ignore him entirely. Surely, she'd politely tell him to piss off if that were the case.

His chest tightened uncomfortably. She was all alone in a foreign country, a country where she didn't even speak the language, and as far as he knew, no one had seen or heard from her now in almost twenty-four hours. What if something had happened?

He wished he knew how to contact one of her friends. Surely, they'd also noticed her lack of social media content today. Probably—hopefully—they even knew the reason why. After he'd tried in vain to concentrate on the comedy on his TV screen for about fifteen minutes, he finally gave in and picked up his phone. Best to call now before it got too late.

It rang three times, long enough that he felt the knot in his chest tighten into real fear, before he heard a click and Ruby's voice.

"I was just about to text you back, you know." She sounded different, like she was congested. He'd never even considered the possibility that she might be sick.

"Is that so?" he asked, trying to keep his tone light so she wouldn't hear how worried he'd been.

"Yes. I was taking a bath, and I was in there longer than I realized. I just saw your message." There was a muffled sound, like she was trying to stifle a cough.

"Are you sick?" he asked.

"Just a cough. I'm okay."

He remembered the night they met when they sat together in the gardens of the Langdon estate, she'd told him about a condition that affected her immune system and how she'd been too sick to attend school as a child. He was under the impression she was much better now, but he also remembered her saying that she still had to be careful about her health. "Is it just a cough?" he asked carefully.

She sighed, as if she'd already been over this a million times, and she probably had, because if he'd been worried, no doubt her friends and family were too. "No, but I went back to the clinic this morning and got chest X-rays and antibiotics. Believe me, I take my health very seriously. When you have a compromised immune system, you don't get to screw around, even with a simple cough. But I've got it all under control."

"Chest X-rays?" That sounded a lot more serious than a simple cough.

"I'm very prone to pneumonia," she told him in a resigned tone. "But we caught it really early. The antibiotics should knock it right out."

"Pneumonia," he repeated. "Ruby..."

"It's really not as bad as it sounds." Behind the hoarseness, her voice was coated in steel. "I've dealt with this so many times, I know the drill by heart."

"Are you flying home early?" he asked.

Another sigh, this time ending in a deep, wracking cough. "I'm actually not allowed to fly right now. Apparently, changes in air pressure in the cabin could be bad for my lungs."

"Is anyone with you?"

"No. I told them the same thing I'm about to tell you. I'm really and truly capable of taking care of myself. I'll be fine, I promise."

"Just because you can doesn't mean you should," he said gently. "And I'm a lot closer than any of your other friends and family. I also have access to a private jet."

Muffled laughter carried over the line. "Of course, you do."

"So?"

"Thank you, but no."

"Would you let me fly one of your friends over to stay with you? Or your mom?"

"You would do that?"

"Of course, I would. I can't stand the thought of you being all alone and sick in Paris. Honestly, I can't believe someone didn't insist on coming over to stay with you."

There was dead silence over the line.

"Ruby, you did tell them you're sick, didn't you?"

"I did," she confirmed.

"Then what?"

"I might have lied and said you were going to check in on me."

"That settles it," he said. "You've already virtually promised me to look after you. If anything were to happen, your family's going to hold me accountable, right? So, I'd better be there to make good on that promise."

"That's ridiculous, you know," she said, but her tone had softened.

"Not at all. I won't get in your way, I promise. I'll even book my own room. But you'll have someone to bring you soup and ride with you if you have to go back to the clinic."

She coughed, and when she spoke again, her voice was raspier than ever. "I'm not at the hotel anymore."

"Where are you?" He sat upright, envisioning her in the hospital, an oxygen tube in her nose and an IV pinned to her hand.

"I booked an Airbnb since I'm going to be stuck here for another two weeks or so," she said quietly. "Now, I have a kitchen and laundry and stuff."

"Would you like me to get a hotel room nearby?" he asked carefully, not wanting to overstep any bounds, since he was already sort of forcing this visit on her.

"No," she whispered. "It's okay. You can stay here with me."

"All right, then. I'll see you tomorrow morning."

10

_____

*R*uby was awakened by the doorbell, confused as she squinted at her phone, because Flynn wasn't supposed to be here for another two hours. But when she shuffled downstairs to the door, a deliveryman stood there with a large paper sack, which he handed to her, speaking rapidly in French. She didn't catch a single word, but the package was warm beneath her fingers, like it contained food.

"*Pardon*," she said, shaking her head. "I didn't order anything. I think you're at the wrong door."

He pointed at the receipt stapled to the bag, which had her name on it, before walking to a blue sedan parked at the curb. Ruby stood there for another moment in confusion before she closed the door and made her way slowly back upstairs to the little one bedroom flat she'd rented here in Paris until she could fly home.

She paused at the top of the stairs, coughing and wheezing while she caught her breath, one hand pressed against her chest. Those stairs were killing her, but unfortunately, she hadn't been able to find a ground floor rental on such short notice.

Once she'd recovered, she bolted the door behind her and carried the package into the kitchen. What was it, and where had it come from? Inside, she found a large plastic container of soup and a loaf of French bread. Her stomach gurgled at the sight. Damn, that looked good. Her first thought was that Flynn had done this, but it could have easily come from her parents, her sister, or even Megan. Ruby knew they were all worrying about her.

And while she was really and truly capable of handling this on her own, she also couldn't deny that it would be nice to have someone else around, someone to hang out with while she was confined to her rented flat, someone to run down to the market and grab food or medicine so she didn't have to go out herself. Plus, it would be good just to see him. She'd missed him…a lot.

If only she was seeing him again for happier reasons. It definitely wasn't ideal to let a man she'd recently slept with for the first time and liked more than anyone she'd dated in recent years to come take care of her when she looked and felt like shit. Her vanity cried at the injustice.

But still, she couldn't wait to see him.

She pulled out a bowl from one of the cabinets and a ladle from the drawer next to the oven and scooped out a bowl of soup. She stirred, inhaling the scent of chicken and herbs. It seemed to be a French approximation of chicken noodle, and it smelled delicious. She pulled up a barstool to the counter and sat, ridiculously glad for a hot meal she hadn't had to prepare herself.

The soup was seasoned in a way she wasn't used to but really liked, despite her compromised appetite. She'd eaten several spoonfuls when her phone began to ring. Her sister Liza's name showed on the screen.

"Hey," she said as she connected the call.

"How are you feeling?" Liza asked.

"Pretty crummy, but nothing unexpected." Ruby sipped from her soup.

"Is Flynn there yet?" she asked.

"No, but he will be soon."

"And you're sure this is what you want? I could fly out. Or Mom. She's having a fit knowing you're stranded over there by yourself, you know."

"I know." Ruby smiled into her soup. Her family knew as well as she did that she could handle a bout with pneumonia, but they worried. They'd always worried about her, and they always would. "Flynn's great, really. I'll be in good hands."

"You like him a lot, huh?" Liza asked.

"I do." Ruby stirred her spoon through the soup, watching as various herbs swirled across the surface. "I'm glad I'll get to see him again before I come home."

"Well, be careful, and call me anytime," Liza said. "And also call me to dish about you and Flynn, once you're feeling a little better."

Ruby laughed, which turned into a fit of coughing. "Will do."

She and Liza wrapped up their conversation, and Ruby finished her soup. After she'd eaten, she took her medication and stood in a long, hot shower, letting the steam help break up the mucous in her lungs. Then, she spent the next fifteen minutes hunched over a box of tissues, coughing it all up. She'd just settled on the couch with her e-reader when the doorbell rang again.

This time, it would be Flynn.

Heat rolled through her belly, generating sparks that pinged through her whole body, flooding her with so much adrenaline that she was able to walk downstairs almost as quickly as a healthy person. She paused at the door, glancing down at her loose T-shirt and leggings, picturing her shower-damp hair and lack of makeup. Well, it couldn't be helped.

She pulled the door open. Flynn stood on her doorstep in

jeans and an emerald green polo shirt, looking so ridiculously handsome her knees actually trembled at the sight.

"Hi," she said.

"Hi." He stepped forward, took her hands in his, and placed a gentle kiss on her cheek. "Thank you for letting me come."

"You didn't leave me much of a choice, did you?" she teased, but she was so glad to see him, she couldn't put any heat into the words. She gestured for him to follow her up the stairs to her flat. He carried a black duffel bag and a briefcase, which he set down inside the door, looking around with interest.

"Nice place."

She leaned against the doorway, taking shallow breaths as she recovered from the exertion of the stairs. "It is, especially considering I needed something so last minute." The flat consisted of an open living space with a couch and a galley kitchen. There was a small row of windows near the ceiling that let in natural light. Two doors on the right-hand side of the room led to the bedroom and bath.

"You look good, all things considered," he said, one hand sliding through her hair to cup her cheek as he looked her over.

"All things considered?" She led the way toward the couch.

"I mean, you're a little pale, but I was expecting you to look a lot sicker than you do." He gave her one of those classic Flynn grins, the kind that had melted her resolve right from the first moment they met.

"I'm not on my deathbed, I promise." She curled up on the couch, pulling a throw blanket over herself as she settled against the pillow she'd put there earlier.

"Shouldn't you be in bed, though?"

She shook her head, gesturing for him to sit with her. "I'm more comfortable here. It's easier to keep my head elevated. If I lay flat, I cough more." As if she'd jinxed herself with the words, she doubled over in a coughing fit, big, wracking coughs that left her gasping for breath.

He sat beside her, rubbing her back until the spasms

subsided. "Can I do anything? Get anything for you?" His gaze fell on the portable oxygen tank by the wall, and alarm flashed in his eyes.

"I don't use it much," she told him. "It helps keep my oxygen levels up if I need to be on my feet for a while."

"Well, you won't need to be now that I'm here," he said resolutely, his hand still resting protectively on her back. "What can I do for you?"

"Water would be nice, actually," she murmured, clearing her throat as another cough bubbled up from her chest.

He stood and went into the kitchen, returning a minute later with a glass of water, which she took gratefully.

"Thank you." She gulped down about half the glass and set it on the table in front of her. "Did you really fly here on a private jet?"

He took her feet and laid them over his lap, adjusting the throw blanket to keep her warm. "I took a charter from Wales to London and flew commercial from there."

"You're so fancy," she whispered with a smile.

He rubbed her feet absently, giving her a tender look. "How are you, really?"

"I'm prone to crap like this," she told him. "As long as I take care of myself, I'll be back on my feet in no time."

He leaned back, seeming to relax as if he'd finally decided she really was going to be okay. "Anything good on?" he asked, tipping his head toward the TV on the far wall.

"It's all in French," she told him with a smile.

"I have my ChromeCast in my bag," he said. "It's a device that lets you send shows and movies from your phone or laptop to the TV. I always bring it with me when I travel."

"I know what a ChromeCast is," she told him in amusement. "You forget I'm a computer geek in my real life. And that sounds great. I'd love to relax and binge-watch TV, but I couldn't find anything in English worth watching."

Flynn got his ChromeCast and plugged it into the TV, but

she insisted that he pick the first movie, because she could already feel herself starting to drift. Sure enough, she barely made it through the opening credits of the historical drama he'd chosen before she fell asleep. When she woke, he made her hot tea and put on one of her favorite romantic comedies.

"Don't you need to be working?" she asked sleepily.

"I worked on the plane, but I'll set up my laptop tomorrow so I can work while I'm here."

"Okay. Don't let me distract you." She reached over to squeeze his fingers.

"I won't."

They spent most of the rest of the day snuggled on the couch together, watching movies as she drifted in and out of sleep. Flynn seemed to spend more time playing on his phone than actually watching the TV, but he never complained. He brought her everything she needed, including all her medication, so she didn't have to leave the couch except to use the bathroom. And even though she could have managed on her own, it was nice, *really* nice, having him here.

"What would you like for dinner?" he asked as she lay against his chest, half-asleep as the credits rolled at the end of *Skyscraper*.

"I'm not that hungry. I could probably just eat more of the soup I had for lunch. Did you send that?"

"I did," he confirmed.

"Thank you. It was delicious," she whispered, fighting the urge to cough. Her chest ached something fierce, and the shivery sensation on her skin meant her fever had returned.

"I'm glad. Anything you want for supper, just name it, and I'll go get it for you."

"Well, I do have a craving for ice cream." She turned her head to look up at him with a smile.

"I read that you shouldn't have dairy products," he told her solemnly. "It can make your body produce more mucous."

"I know that." Had he researched pneumonia to help take

care of her? *Gah.* She was so screwed where he was concerned. She sat up and grabbed a tissue off the table to cough into. "Sounds so good right now, though."

"What about sorbet?" he asked. "Or a fruit smoothie?"

"Mm." She leaned back on the couch, closing her eyes. "A smoothie sounds fantastic, actually."

"Say no more." He leaned over, pressing his lips against her neck with a quick, gentle kiss that filled her with a combination of heat and chills. Desire and fevers really didn't mix.

"Thanks, Flynn," she whispered, snuggling into the blanket on the couch as he left the flat. She had no idea how long he was gone, because she was asleep almost before he was out the door. The next thing she knew, he was back with a paper bag and a plastic smoothie cup. "Oh my God, you're the best."

She took the smoothie from him and sipped gratefully. It felt like heaven going down her raw, parched throat. He set several containers of food on the glass table in front of the couch and went into the kitchen for plates and utensils.

"I got a few different things," he said as he rummaged through cabinets. "I figured leftovers are going to be our friend this week."

"Definitely," she agreed, still sipping from her smoothie.

They chatted comfortably as they ate, then watched a documentary on Netflix before she was ready to call it a night.

"Would you like me to go to a hotel nearby?" he asked. "Or I can sleep out here on the couch, if you prefer."

"I'm happy to share the bedroom with you." She leaned over, pressing her lips against his cheek. "And I'm not contagious, by the way. But I might keep you up all night coughing. The couch pulls out if you'd rather sleep here."

His arms went around her, lifting her from the couch to carry her into the bedroom. "I would rather sleep with you."

Flynn woke to the sound of Ruby coughing in bed beside him, reaching over instinctively to rub her back before he stood to refill her glass of water.

"Thank you," she whispered, squinting at him adorably without her glasses. She took the glass and drank, wincing as she pressed a hand to her chest.

"Anything else you need?"

She shook her head, taking shallow breaths until the spasms had passed. Weak daylight filtered in through the windows, telling him that morning had arrived. He leaned back, drawing her against his chest, and she snuggled in without protest, wrapping an arm around him. Her skin was feverishly warm against his, her breaths still shallow and ragged.

"I'm glad you're here," she whispered.

"Me too." He'd wanted to see her again so badly, and while he really wished she weren't sick, he was so glad that he could be here for her. And with her.

They lay there like that for a while, dozing and holding each other, before they finally got up. Ruby spent the day on the couch, alternately napping and watching TV, while he worked at his laptop at the desk in the corner. It felt disconcertingly comfortable, domestic even. And as much as he was glad to be here helping her, he had to grudgingly admit she'd had a pretty good handle on things on her own.

There was a chart pinned to the fridge with her daily medication schedule, including probiotics and vitamins, each one dutifully checked off after she'd taken it.

"Weren't you supposed to be taking a break from lists on this trip?" he asked jokingly as he brought over her antibiotic and a glass of water.

She narrowed her eyes at him. "That rule pertained to my trip. I wanted to have an uncharted adventure, but I don't mess around with my health."

"I'd say you've had quite an uncharted adventure." He

leaned over to kiss her cheek as a wave of affection barreled through him.

Ruby snuggled into her blanket nest on the couch, smiling up at him from behind her glasses. Her hair was kind of a mess, her face makeup free and pale from her illness, and yet she looked so lovely, he could hardly draw breath. "I suppose I have," she said. "I certainly didn't see this coming."

His phone began to ring. He swiped it from his pocket to reveal his mother's name on the screen. "Be right back," he told Ruby before he stepped into the bedroom and connected the call. "Hello, Mother."

"Hello, darling," she said. "I hear you're in Paris?"

"And how did you hear that?" he asked, running a hand through his hair as he paced toward the window, wishing it was low enough to look out of. He felt a sudden kinship with the animals at the zoo, looking for a way out of their enclosures.

"Your father and Aidan spoke today about financial matters, and he mentioned you'd run off on him, chased a girl to Paris."

"I didn't run off on him. I had completed all the surveying work and gone over the initial renderings with him when a friend became ill, and I flew out to stay with her for a few days while she recuperates. Aidan's project is proceeding according to schedule."

"It's just that you have a habit of doing this, Flynn. You lose focus before you've completed a project."

"I've got everything under control, Mother." He didn't add that Aidan was the one who'd first suggested Flynn come to Paris, knowing that was beside the point his mother was trying to make. "I'll be finished with this project on time, and I'll be in Dubai on the first to begin work there."

"All right, then. So, who is this friend you're caring for?"

"Ruby Keller. You met her briefly at the Langdon wedding last week."

"Oh? I thought you two had only just met that night."

"We did, but we've remained in touch. She came down with pneumonia, and since she was so far from home, I offered to give her a hand while she's recovering."

"That's very sweet of you," his mother said. "Just be careful that you don't get distracted from your work, that's all."

11

The sounds of the city awakened her, cars humming down the street outside and a church bell clanging in the distance. Ruby stretched, opening her eyes to peer at her surroundings. The blurry living room of the flat in Paris appeared in front of her, which meant she'd dozed off on the couch. Sometimes, it was hard to remember whether it was day or night when she slept so much. The one constant was Flynn, and there he was now, handing her glasses to her.

She slid them onto her face, and the room came into focus. "Thank you. What time is it?"

"Just past noon." He sat beside her on the couch. "Feeling any better?"

"Yeah." She pushed herself into a sitting position. This was the fifth day since starting antibiotics, the fourth day since Flynn's arrival, and the medication was definitely starting to take effect. Her fever was gone, and her cough was beginning to ease.

"Ready for lunch?" he asked.

"Sure." She wasn't particularly hungry, but she knew she needed to eat to aid her recovery. "What do we have today?"

"I picked up some bread, meats, and cheese at the market

this morning. I thought we could make a light meal out of it, if that sounds good to you."

"It sounds perfect." She sat up, coughing. "And actually, what do you think about making it a picnic?"

"A picnic?" A wrinkle appeared between his brows as he processed her request.

She rubbed at her chest as the coughing subsided. "There's an adorable little park at the end of the block. I saw it when the taxi dropped me off."

"I don't know if that's a good idea."

"Some fresh air would be good for me," she said. "We can bring a blanket and lay in the park for a little while. I'll even use my oxygen tank for the walk."

He looked like he was going to argue with her about it, but after a moment, he reached over and squeezed her hand. "If you're sure it's okay, I'd be happy to fix us a picnic."

"I'm sure it's okay," she whispered. "I need to be really careful about exposing myself to germs right now, so I'll only sit on our blanket, but I need some fresh air. If I were at home, I would have spent a lot of time outside, resting in the yard."

"All right, then." Flynn got up and went into the kitchen.

Ruby peeled herself off the couch and went to make herself presentable. She brushed her hair and clipped it back, splashed some water on her face, and put on a bra under her T-shirt. She sat on the bed to put on her sneakers and then went into the living room to get her oxygen tank.

Flynn had a paper grocery bag in one hand and a duffel bag in the other. "Do you need help with that?"

She shook her head as she slipped the cannula into place across her nose and behind her ears and started the oxygen flowing. When she'd finished, she rolled the tank across the room to join him, smirking at the barely disguised concern on his face.

"You're sure this is okay?" His gaze darted from the tank to her face.

"I'm positive," she assured him. "Believe me, I want to get well as quickly as possible so I can get out of here and go home." Except as she said it, she realized it wasn't true. As much as she hated being sick and stranded in Paris, she liked being here with him. Her words hung in the air between them. Flynn's gaze dropped to the floor, a sort of deflated air around him.

She stepped forward and pressed her lips against his. "But I'm really glad I'm here with you right now."

He set down their picnic, his arms sliding around her waist to tuck her in against his chest. "I am too."

She turned her face against the soft cotton of his T-shirt. Flynn was tall and solidly built, so much so that her head fit neatly below his chin. She should have felt small in his arms, frail even, given the oxygen tank she was attached to. But she didn't. Something about the way he held her just felt...right.

They stood like that for a minute, holding on to each other. His heart thumped steadily beneath her ear. Finally, she stepped back. Flynn turned and opened the door to the hall. He glanced at the flight of stairs that led to the street below before turning back to her.

And then, as if he'd just made a decision, he lifted the oxygen tank and handed it to her. She clutched it against her chest, opening her mouth to ask him what the hell he was doing, but he'd already swept her into his arms and was carrying her down the stairs.

"No stairs for you," he said simply as he set her down. "Not until you can walk without that thing."

"Um. Okay." She couldn't fight the smile that tugged at her lips as he jogged back up the stairs to get the bags containing their picnic. She would have protested the act of bravado, except the stairs really had done a number on her the last time she'd scaled them. And besides, she already knew he wasn't prone to acts of bravado. Acts of kindness, though? Yeah, he was a master.

They walked outside together. Sunlight washed over her, and she squinted, feeling like a bear coming out of hibernation. The breeze tickled her skin, and she tilted her face toward the sky, soaking up the sun's warmth. Yes, this was exactly what she'd needed.

Flynn's free hand found its way into hers, and they strolled toward the park at a leisurely pace. The wheels on the tank rattled over the uneven chunks of pavement beneath them, providing the soundtrack for their walk.

"Tell me if you need to stop and rest," he said, giving her hand a squeeze.

She just squeezed it back, because although she was one hundred percent enjoying the fresh air and the walk, it was probably best to save all her breath for the task at hand. The street curved slightly to the right, and the park came into sight. It was nothing much, just a little square of green between two street corners. Benches lined its edges, and a statue in the middle was flanked by beds of red and purple flowers.

They crossed the street and made their way over to it. An elderly couple sat together on one of the benches, but otherwise, the park was deserted. Flynn opened his duffel bag and pulled out a blue blanket, which he spread across the grass. Gratefully, she sat, crossing her legs in front of herself. She was a bit winded from the walk, but her blood was pumping in a good way. She felt energized and alive, grateful for this beautiful Parisian day and Flynn's company.

Pneumonia could look so much worse than this. She knew firsthand, and she'd take this beautiful park and this handsome man over a hospital bed any day of the week.

He opened the other bag and began spreading out their picnic. And while she hadn't had much of an appetite since getting sick, her stomach actually grumbled in anticipation. He laid out meat, cheese, bread, and even a sprig of plump purple grapes, followed by two bottles of sparkling water.

"It'll have to do until you're off the antibiotics," he said with a wink as he handed her a bottle.

"It's perfect." She screwed off the top and took a long drink. "How is your friend's house coming along?" she asked as they began to prepare their plates.

"Really well," he told her, his face an interesting contradiction of emotions. She saw excitement and pride mixed with something less happy, almost dark. Flynn was a paradox that way, and she still hadn't quite figured out the source of his melancholy where work was concerned.

"Would you show it to me?" she asked. "Once we're back at the flat?"

He looked up at her, surprise evident in the rise of his eyebrows. "I'd be glad to."

"Cool." She bit off a chunk of crusty bread, crunching it thoughtfully. "I have no idea how that process works, and I'd love to see what you're working on."

"Well, I'll draw up the plans for the house, conferring with Aidan on all the particulars, and once he's signed off on everything, we'll deliver the final design to the builder."

"And this is what you enjoy doing?" she asked. "Do you prefer it to work at the hotel?"

He rolled a slice of salami around a wedge of cheese and popped it into his mouth, chewing and swallowing before he answered. "I'm not sure how to answer that, exactly. But yes, this is my favorite thing to do, designing something from scratch."

"You don't get to do that at Exeter," she guessed. "The hotels have standards that they follow, guidelines."

"Exactly."

"Have you thought of opening your own architecture business?"

"I've thought about it." He took another bite.

"Would your family be upset about you leaving the business? Couldn't you still work with them while having your own clients?" She created her own meat and cheese roll-up and popped it in her mouth.

"I'm not sure I have it in me to be a business owner."

"Why not?" she pressed.

"I sometimes have trouble seeing things through to completion. I lose interest. It's why I've been placed on so many different projects. My mother doesn't think—"

"She's wrong," Ruby interrupted softly. "I don't think you have any trouble seeing things through, not if they're important things or things that truly interest you."

He looked away, a muscle twitching in his cheek. "I'm not sure you've known me long enough to say that with any authority."

"Fair point," she conceded. "But I don't foresee you having any trouble seeing me through my recuperation or finishing Aidan's project on time. Maybe the work you're doing at Exeter just isn't right for you."

"Maybe."

She'd seen a bit of what he meant, though. She'd noticed the way his attention wandered during movies, how he seemed to flit from task to task in the kitchen. He'd been nonstop when they toured London together, and he seemed to focus with laser-like intensity when he worked on the mock-up for Aidan's new house. "Please feel free to tell me if I'm way out of line, but have you ever been tested for ADHD?"

His gaze snapped to hers. "Why do you ask?"

"My sister has it. She struggled a lot in school, and it made her feel stupid when the opposite was true. People think it means you can't focus, but you can. People with ADHD are hyper-focused on the things that interest them. You just remind me of her that way, that's all."

"I was diagnosed in secondary school," he said, still staring off into the distance.

"Oh." She hugged her knees against her chest. "Well, then you already know everything I just said."

"I guess I had forgotten the part about being able to focus on things that interest you," he said. "Although, I'm not sure that's true in my case."

"I've seen you focus on a lot of things. In fact, I don't think I would have even noticed it if not for my sister's experience." She paused, gauging his response to her words. "What I noticed more is your perception of yourself. I think that sometimes you don't go after what you really want, because you're afraid you'll mess it up, but you underestimate yourself, Flynn."

He reached over and gave her hand a squeeze. "I appreciate the vote of confidence, but you've never really seen me at work."

"True." She squeezed back. "But I still think you can do anything you want, if you decide to stop holding yourself back."

Flynn was quiet, his expression troubled.

"Secondary school is late to be diagnosed," she commented.

"It is," he agreed.

"Did you have trouble in school because of it?"

"It wasn't easy," he admitted. "I'm the youngest, as you know, and my siblings all excelled in school. My parents didn't understand why I couldn't just sit down and finish my lessons like they did or why my marks were always so low."

"I'm sorry." Her heart ached for young Flynn, trying and failing to live up to his parents' expectations. Obviously, he'd internalized those feelings and carried them with him into adulthood. "I wish you'd had more support when you were younger."

"I think I turned out all right anyway," he said with a playful smile, clearly trying to lighten the mood.

"You turned out more than all right."

He took her empty plate from her and began packing up the remains of their picnic. She tugged the oxygen tube out of her nose and lay back on the blanket, eyes closed, soaking up the warmth of the sun overhead.

"This is perfection," she whispered.

"I'm glad."

She heard fabric shuffling and then Flynn was beside her, his hand sliding into hers. Birds twittered overhead, and the pungent scent of flowers filled her nose. "This isn't how I planned to see Paris, but it's not so bad."

"You're getting a different flavor for the city than you would have as a tourist, that's for sure," he agreed.

"Maybe I'll come back sometime and do the tourist thing properly."

"You absolutely should."

"It's so good to get out of the flat. Truthfully, I'm starting to get a little stir-crazy watching TV all day. I really wish I had my laptop or my Nintendo to give me something else to do."

"That's the problem with getting sick when you're away from home, isn't it?" Flynn said.

She nodded against the blanket. "You've been a nice distraction, though."

They lay together in the sunshine. Peace flowed through her, something she wasn't used to feeling in a situation like this. Usually, she drew contentment from crossing off all the items on her to-do list before bed, feeling that she'd accomplished everything she set out to do that day. She'd done absolutely nothing today, but somehow it didn't seem to matter, because it just felt right being here with Flynn.

Her feelings for him were growing much stronger than she should have ever let them, given that they had to say goodbye soon. His life was here in England, and hers was in Virginia. She wasn't prepared to give that up for a man, no matter how much she liked him. And she really did like him a *lot*. But maybe…was it so crazy to try a long-distance relationship, at least for a little while, just to see what happened?

She rolled to face him, studying his profile. The unruly lock of dark hair that tended to flop over his forehead was behaving at the moment as he lay on his back, tamed by gravity. Stubble darkened his cheeks, and she reached over to touch it, letting her fingers skim over his skin. His stubble prickled against her fingertips, sending a delicious shiver through her body.

She leaned in, replacing her fingers with her lips. His scruff tickled, but beneath it, his skin was warm and soft against hers. He turned his head, and their lips met.

"Hard to believe we've only known each other a week," she murmured against his mouth.

He rolled onto his side, cupping a hand against her cheek, the expression in his eyes fierce yet tender. "Sometimes, when we meet someone, it feels like we've known them forever. I felt that with you from the moment we met."

"I did too." She kissed him again, scooting closer to him on the blanket.

"I think that's a connection we'll always have, even after we go home."

RUBY DIDN'T PROTEST WHEN FLYNN CARRIED HER UP THE STAIRS to their flat an hour later. She stowed her oxygen tank against the wall and stretched, invigorated by the blood flowing through her veins, more energized than she had been in days. "That felt so good. I think we should do it again tomorrow."

"I'd like that," Flynn said, moving to the kitchen to put away their leftovers.

"I feel bad that you're always having to take care of the chores around here," she said, watching as he threw away their picnic trash. "I'll be able to help out more soon."

"Don't," he told her. "It's not as though I've been spending hours in the kitchen cooking for you." It was true. They'd mostly ordered takeout, although he'd also kept them stocked with food from the market around the corner. "I don't often get the chance to do this for someone. It's good to feel useful."

"Well, thank you. Really."

At Flynn's insistence, she lay down in bed to rest, and the next thing she knew, the ringing of her phone jostled her from a deep sleep. Apparently, all that sunshine had tired her out. Without her glasses, she couldn't read the name on the display screen, but no doubt it was one of her friends or family calling to check in. "Hello."

"Hi," Megan said. "I didn't wake you, did I?"

Ruby cleared her throat, coughing. "Just napping, no worries."

"Ah, crap. I should have texted first, shouldn't I?"

"No," Ruby told her honestly. "I'm glad to hear your voice."

"How are things? Feeling any better?"

"I am. In fact, Flynn and I walked down to a little park nearby earlier. It felt so good to get out of this damn flat, but I guess it tired me out."

"Well, that's good. Any word yet on when you'll be able to fly home?"

"Best case scenario is next week," Ruby told her. "I have a follow-up appointment at the clinic tomorrow to see how my lungs are doing, but I think I'm making good progress. I might just have to be one of those people who wears a mask on the plane and bathes in hand sanitizer to keep from exposing myself to any unnecessary germs during the flight."

"Oh God, I didn't think of that," Megan exclaimed. "We'll have to fully decontaminate you when you get off the plane. Actually, let me talk to Theo when he and Elle get home from their honeymoon. I'm sure he could send the Langdon jet for you. That has to be more sanitary than a commercial flight."

"You know, that's not a bad idea." Ordinarily, Ruby felt uncomfortable using Theo's wealth to her own advantage, but having a private jet at her disposal would undoubtedly allow her to come home sooner. But did she want to come home sooner? Or did she want to stay here with Flynn? Of course, he had to leave soon to fly to Dubai.

One way or another, their cozy time together here in Paris

was coming to an end, sooner than either of them might be ready for.

"Elle and Theo will be home on Sunday, and I'll mention it to him then," Megan said.

"I appreciate it." She stared up at the vaulted ceiling overhead, watching shadows play across it from the trees outside her window.

"I've got to get ready for a photography session, but I'll check in with you later."

"Thanks, Meg." She said goodbye and ended the call, laying for a few minutes while her thoughts swirled in a million different directions. Somehow, after all this, she wasn't ready for her trip to end, wasn't ready to go home. But she was getting ahead of herself. She had at least another week in Paris before her lungs would be healed enough to fly.

So, she got out of bed, went into the bathroom to freshen up, and headed into the living room to find Flynn. He was—as she expected—sitting at the desk against the wall, hard at work on his design for Aidan.

"Can I see?" she asked as she walked up behind him.

"Of course." He stood, motioning for her to take the chair. "Did you have a nice nap?"

"I did. I've gotten awfully used to being lazy all day," she told him with a self-deprecating smile as she sat.

"I don't think that's going to be a problem for you once you're well."

"No?"

He shook his head. "I get the impression you're a very driven woman, and I think you're already itching to get back to your busy life."

"You might be right about that." Despite her reluctance to leave Flynn—and Paris—behind, she missed her friends and her life at Rosemont Castle. "It'll be good to go home. I've never been away from my cats this long before. I really miss them."

"Cats, huh?"

"Simon and Oliver." She swiped the screen on her phone and scrolled through her camera roll until she came to a selfie she'd taken a few days before she left for London. "That's Simon sprawled across my lap, and Oliver's laying next to me. He likes to be close, but he's not a lap cat."

"Pretty cats," Flynn commented.

"They're Siamese. Littermates. Someone found them in a bag in a garbage can in downtown Orlando. They were the only two to survive."

"That's awful."

"It happens all the time, unfortunately," she told him. "At least, it does in America. Maybe things are different here."

"I doubt it. Humanity is what it is," he said with a frown.

"You're probably right. Anyway, I volunteered at the shelter on weekends during college, and I was there when they came in. I took them home to bottle feed them, and by the time they were old enough to be adopted, I decided to adopt them myself."

"That's quite a story," Flynn said, leaning a hip against the desk. "I've never had a pet, I'm afraid."

"Never?"

"Never."

"Do you like cats, though?"

"I don't not like them."

"Well, I suppose that's a good enough answer." She nudged him playfully. "I don't think we could see each other again if you didn't like my cats."

Flynn's eyes darted to hers, and for a moment, they just stared at each other. "I'm sure I would like them quite a lot," he said finally. But he'd probably never get the chance to meet them, a point she had just inadvertently driven home for both of them.

"Anyway, tell me what I'm looking at." She gestured to the screen in front of her, where she could see blueprints for the house he was designing, hoping to diffuse the suddenly melancholy mood between them.

"I have to go to Dubai, Ruby," he said quietly.

"I know you do. And I have to go home to Virginia."

"I wish it weren't that way."

"Me too." She threaded her fingers through his, remembering her thoughts from the park. "But we've come a long way since we met, when we thought we'd only get that one day together in London. Maybe we should try to find an excuse to see each other again after we go home."

"I'm not sure it would be wise," he said, eyes downcast.

"No?"

"I'm a man who's always on the move, Ruby. I don't think I could make a long-distance relationship work."

She forced a smile. Where were these feelings coming from anyway? She'd barely started thinking about the possibility of a long-distance relationship, but now that she'd thrown the idea out there and he'd rejected it, she felt a crushing disappointment. "Maybe I just meant we could stay friends. But anyway, show me the house."

Flynn leaned in, pointing to the screen. "This is a two-story, contemporary style home, but I wanted to incorporate the feel of the area." He clicked the mouse, bringing up a gallery of photos. "See these pictures? This is the home site in the Wye River Valley in Wales."

"Wow." The home site itself was wooded, overlooking a lush green valley, which sloped down to the river at the bottom. Its hillsides were dotted with quaint little houses. "It's stunning."

"I thought so too. I wanted to make sure Aidan's house maximized his views of the valley and also blended in with its surroundings." He spent the next thirty minutes showing her every detail, from the floor-to-ceiling windows in the master bedroom to the enormous deck overlooking the valley. His final rendering showed a house built of a reddish wood with white trim, rustic and almost antique-looking, while also undeniably sleek and modern in its design.

"Flynn, this is really something. I mean…not that I doubted your talents or anything, but you've created something really unique and beautiful, and from what you've told me, it also suits exactly what Aidan's looking for."

A wide smile broke over Flynn's face, so unabashedly pleased and proud that it melted her heart into a gooey lovesick mess inside her chest. "You really think so?"

"I do. It's amazing." *You should be doing this full time instead of overseeing the construction of hotels that all look exactly the same.* But it wasn't her place to tell him what he should do with his life. After all, family ties were important and strong, and only Flynn could decide if and when to break free of them.

She returned to the couch, buzzing with a kind of restless energy that had been building inside her over the last day or two. She really needed something to do now that she was starting to feel better, or she was going to go crazy cooped up in this apartment.

"I went shopping while you were asleep," Flynn said, closing his laptop and joining her on the couch.

"Oh yeah? What's for dinner?"

"Not that kind of shopping." He reached into a paper bag beside the couch and pulled out a Nintendo Switch.

Ruby gaped at him and then at the gaming console in his hands. "You bought a Switch?"

"Yes. I thought you could show me how to play."

"Really?" She couldn't contain the grin she felt spreading across her face.

"I was curious after hearing you talk about video games." He handed her the box, shamelessly letting her take the lead in setting it up.

Thirty minutes later, they were seated side by side, each holding a joy-con while she kicked his butt in Mario Kart. She laughed until her lungs ached when Flynn got taken out by a

Goomba. God, she'd missed this so much. She hadn't even realized how much until the console was back in her hands.

"Oh no." He threw his hands in the air as his cart spun out on the track, but he was smiling. "I'm rubbish at this game."

"Like all things, it takes practice." And she had a feeling they'd be getting a lot of practice over the next week, both at the game and at playing house here in Paris. How was she ever going to let him go when the time came?

12

———

"*W*ill you stop fussing?"

Flynn raised his hands in surrender as Ruby huffed past him into the stairwell. Part of him wanted an excuse to sweep her into his arms and carry her down the way he'd done the first time they'd gone to the park together, but that had been over a week ago, and she was much better now, almost entirely recovered, in fact. And he was so glad for it, despite it meaning their time together was coming to an end.

"Have you got your mask?" he asked as Ruby pushed open the door that led onto the street.

"Yes," she told him with exaggerated sweetness. He knew she appreciated his fussing as much as she also felt frustrated by it. "I'll put it on when we get there."

"Perfect." He stepped ahead of her to the car idling at the curb and spoke briefly with the driver, confirming their itinerary for the day before opening the rear door for Ruby.

She slid inside with a smile, energy and excitement radiating off her. Yesterday, she'd finished her antibiotics and been given a clean bill of health by the doctor she'd been seeing here in France. Her immune system was still compromised, and her lungs were weak, so she had to take it easy, but more or less, she was back to the same Ruby he'd met at Theo's wedding almost three weeks ago.

"You know, hanging out with you does have its perks," she told him with a wink as the car slid away from the curb.

"I'm glad." Public transportation was out of the question while she was so vulnerable to germs, so he'd chartered a car to take them around the city today. In fact, he'd spared no expense to make sure they enjoyed a fun but quiet day that in no way risked her health.

"And I'm not just talking about the fancy car," she said, her tone gone serious.

"I know."

"I wish I didn't have to go home tomorrow. I mean…I'm so ready to go home, but I'll miss you."

"About that," he said. "My father has a business associate in Washington DC that he asked me to check in with before I head to Dubai. How would you feel about me flying over with you? We could spend a night together in Virginia before I head up to DC."

Ruby gave him a wide smile, eyes brimming with affection. "I would love that."

"All right, then."

She hadn't mentioned a long-distance relationship again since the afternoon he'd shown her the plans for Aidan's house, but he felt her mood dampen every time either of them mentioned going home. In truth, he felt the same way. He wished they could live in this faux domestic bliss forever. But, at the same time, he was already itching to get moving again, to get back to Wales and check in with Aidan, to get on with his project in Dubai. And that was exactly the reason he could never ask Ruby to take a chance on him, no matter how much it would hurt to let her go.

She chattered excitedly the rest of the way to the Eiffel Tower, practically bouncing in her seat. When the car slid to a stop in front of the grand lawns that led to the landmark, she let out a little gasp. "Wow. It looks…smaller than I was expecting."

"I thought the same thing the first time I saw it."

Dutifully, she reached into her bag and put on the purple mask they'd gotten at the pharmacy earlier that week. It covered her nose and mouth, protecting her from germs. Still, they weren't going inside any public spaces today that might put her at risk. He gathered the bag containing their picnic and climbed out of the car, coming around to open her door for her.

"A girl could get used to this, you know." She gripped his hand as she stood, eyes darting around to take in their surroundings.

"Perhaps American men need to try harder to impress."

"Oh, they definitely do. Let's go a little closer before we spread out our blanket." She led the way across the grass, a bounce in her step that he hadn't seen since the day they'd spent together in London.

They chose an open spot on the grass and laid everything out for their picnic. Today, they'd brought sandwiches from the deli down the street.

"How long will you be in Dubai?" Ruby asked as she ate, having taken the mask off for the task.

"About six months."

"That's a long time. I hope you like it there."

"I do too."

"I'll be glad to get back to Rosemont Castle," she said, a wistful note creeping into her tone.

"I bet."

She finished her sandwich, and he leaned over to kiss her before helping her tug the mask back into place.

"This thing is such a mood killer," she murmured from behind it, her eyes full of heat but also humor.

"It is," he agreed. "But also necessary."

"Well, at least you'll have the Switch to keep you company

in Dubai," she said, eyes crinkling behind her glasses as she smiled.

"And I did beat you at Mario Kart that one time, which means I'm not completely hopeless."

"You're pretty good at Zelda, actually," she told him. "With a little more practice, you might even catch up to me."

"I quite like that one." He hadn't gotten the hang of all the games she'd shown him, but he liked the adventure quest format of Zelda. "I'll definitely keep playing."

"I'm glad. Where will you go after Dubai?" she asked, leaning back on her elbows to look up at the Eiffel Tower looming over them.

"I don't know yet. There's talk of sending me to San Francisco to oversee renovations to the location there."

She was quiet for a long minute, staring up at the tower. "Maybe I could come out for a visit."

"As a friend?" he asked, his chest filled with a combination of lust and longing and regret.

She turned her head to meet his eyes. "If that's what you want me to be."

"It's not what I want you to be," he said quietly, "but it's the only thing you can be. I wander the globe with Exeter. It's what I do and what I enjoy. And we both know this thing between us was never meant to be a 'casual hookup when I'm in town' kind of relationship. You're meant for something so much more than that."

"So are you," she murmured.

"I don't know that I am." The thought of getting married, of settling down had always frightened him. What if he lost interest in his wife the way he seemed to do with everything else?

"You are," she told him with absolute certainty in her voice. "I've seen you, Flynn. The real you, not the version of yourself you show your parents. Have you ever considered that you live up—or down, more like—to their expectations when you're around them? They shuffle you around because they think you're flighty, so you always hold something back, you let yourself wander because you don't see any point in building anything permanent when you've always got one foot out the door anyway."

"I—" He shook his head.

"Just make sure you aren't underestimating yourself."

He didn't know what to say to that. After all, Ruby had only known him for a few weeks and under special circumstances. Then again, he was who he was, even in small doses.

They sat on their blanket for a while, talking and people-watching while they soaked up the nice weather and scenic surroundings. When they finally packed up, he texted their driver, who met them at the curb. They spent the afternoon touring Paris that way, driving by most of the locations Ruby had wanted to see. They got out of the car to take pictures, but they stayed outside where the air was fresh.

They saw the Arc de Triomphe, the Louvre, and any number of other landmarks. At the Saint Chappelle cathedral, Ruby insisted they go inside so she could get a taste of the history before she left Paris. He went ahead to pre-purchase their tickets so she wouldn't have to wait in line. Inside, they climbed a spiral staircase to reach the sanctuary of the church, taking in the steepled ceiling overhead, light filtering in soft hues around them from the vivid stained-glass windows that reached far above their heads.

"It's so gorgeous," she murmured, tugging her mask down for a moment so he could take a picture of her standing at the center of the cathedral. She'd resurrected her #RubyGoes-Rogue hashtag earlier this week, at first just posting photos from the park near their flat and even a few of them playing video games together. "Putting my hashtag to good use today," she said as she posted the picture.

"I'm glad."

After they left Saint Chappelle, Ruby fake-pouted in the

back of the car, thinking they were returning to the flat for dinner. "What do you want to pick up tonight?"

"We're not going back to the flat," he told her with a wink.

"Ooh, a surprise!" She grinned at him. "Does it involve dinner?"

"It does."

"But not at the flat?"

He shook his head, watching the delighted expression on her face as she processed this information. It filled him with something warm and light, an impossibly pleasant sensation.

"Well, whatever it is, I already know I'm going to love it," she whispered, leaning in to kiss his cheek.

The car drove across downtown, pulling to a stop in front of a classic stone-fronted building. The sign out front had the restaurant's name, Coquette, in white on a royal blue background. Inside, he could see more color, each wall a different hue. The look and feel of the place had originally drawn his attention, reminding him of Ruby's personality, but the private room upstairs had sealed the deal.

"Oh, Flynn," she whispered as they got out of the car. Ruby hadn't had a single meal outside of the flat—apart from their picnics—since she got sick.

"Don't worry. I made sure this would be safe for you."

"I never doubted that," she told him as she followed him toward the front door. She stood back, allowing him to open the door for her, not touching anything.

He gave his name to the hostess, and she led them upstairs to the room he'd rented for the evening. In this case, the pictures he'd seen on the internet hadn't done it justice. The walls up here were a warm golden yellow, and the night sky had been painted on the ceiling above, giving the impression that they were dining under the stars.

A table for two had been set up in front of the window, a candle gleaming in its center next to a small vase filled with red flowers.

Tears welled in Ruby's eyes as she sat across from him. "You've really outdone yourself tonight."

"Well, let's wait and see if the food's any good," he told her playfully.

"I'm sure it will be. I haven't had anything yet here in Paris that I didn't like."

Their waiter came to check on them, and they ordered a bottle of wine and two cups of soup to start. Ruby excused herself to the bathroom to wash up before she ate, always responsible despite her desire to seize every opportunity for adventure that presented itself.

"I feel a little bit underdressed for this place," she told him as she sat across from him, hands still pink from their recent scrubbing. She had on a blue floor-length sun dress and black sandals.

"You're perfect," he told her, and he didn't just mean her outfit.

The waiter brought their wine and soup, and they ordered entrées. Ruby got a seafood dish while he went for steak. She lifted her wineglass and tapped it against his. "To dinners out, with wine, because your sickly date finally finished her antibiotics."

"If you mean my incredibly strong, resilient date who just kicked pneumonia's ass, then yes, I'll drink to that." He lifted the glass to his lips and sipped.

Ruby did the same, a happy sigh escaping her lips. "The wine is so good here. Everything is so good here."

And he didn't think she meant just the food either.

"I'm really glad you're coming with me tomorrow," she said, reaching out to take his hand across the table.

"I am too. You know, I've known Theo my whole life, but I've never been to Rosemont Castle. I'd say I'm overdue to visit, wouldn't you?"

"Definitely." She sipped her wine, a thoughtful look on her

face. "Elle told me Theo's putting together a dinner for us all tomorrow night."

"Is he?" Flynn was glad for the chance to sit down with his and Ruby's mutual friends, although it might make his departure even more difficult when the time came.

Their entrées arrived then, and they chatted casually as they ate. Outside the window, sunset fell across the Parisian sky, bathing it in deep blues and purples behind the endless network of buildings that spanned the skyline.

"It's so pretty," Ruby said, following his gaze.

"It sure is."

"Virginia's pretty too. In fact, you should be just in time to enjoy peak foliage in the Appalachian forest. There are some great trails around the castle grounds. I can't wait to show you."

"I've seen photos of the kind of foliage you get in America, but I haven't seen it for myself."

"Perfect," she said. "You're in for a treat."

After they'd finished their meals, he asked for a dessert menu.

"Who says I have room for dessert?" Ruby asked with a twinkle in her eye that said she'd never pass up dessert on a night like this and loved that he already knew this about her.

"Just a hunch," he told her.

In the end, they shared a plate of macarons as they finished off their bottle of wine.

"Mm. Okay, now I'm stuffed." She wiped a pink crumb from her bottom lip and rubbed her stomach dramatically. "I'm so glad I got to go out for one nice meal while I was here. It was everything I could have wanted for my last night in Paris."

Outside the window of the Langdon private jet, the sun shone blindingly bright. Below them, puffy clouds drifted over the endless expanse of the ocean. Ruby leaned back in her seat, relaxing into the soft leather as she stretched her legs out in front of herself. "I could get used to this."

Flynn gave her a knowing look. "Flying commercial has been ruined for you forever."

"You still do, though, right?" She remembered him saying he'd taken a commercial flight from London to Paris to meet her.

"But I fly first class," he said, raising his eyebrows at her.

"Ugh, you're so annoyingly rich," she muttered, but there was no heat to her words, because they both knew she didn't find anything about him annoying, rich or not.

"And yet, it's not my private jet we're flying on today," he commented.

She smiled. "Right. It's actually *my* connection with the Earl of Highcastle that got us this flight."

"I could have asked him too," he reminded her.

"But you didn't. I did."

"Details."

She turned her head and kissed him, sliding her tongue over his bottom lip to taste the salty flavor of his skin. His hand cupped the back of her head, drawing her closer as he deepened the kiss. She and Flynn had kissed a lot during their time together in Paris, mostly chaste kisses, expressing affection more than desire while she was sick. This wasn't a sickbed kiss, though. This kiss was full of fire and passion, fingers grasping at fabric and tongues tangling.

They hadn't had sex since that first night in London, although tonight she hoped that might change. She wanted an amazing night of farewell sex, and this kiss left little doubt that Flynn wanted the same thing.

His hand dropped to her breast, finding and pinching her nipple beneath the combined layers of her dress and bra. "How're your lungs?"

"Pulling in more air than they have in weeks," she whispered, sucking in a deep breath as his hand wandered down her stomach.

"That's good news." His voice was deep and gravelly, the way it sounded during sex, igniting a throbbing ache between her thighs.

She gasped as he cupped her through her dress. "Flynn…"

"Tell me what you want."

"You, in my bed tonight."

"Yes." He captured her mouth for another blistering kiss. "Anything you want, as long as you're feeling up for it."

"Oh, I'm up for it." She glanced over and saw the tent in the front of his pants. "And I don't think I'm the only one."

He chuckled, stroking her through the thin cotton of her dress. "Definitely up."

"Tonight feels like a long way off," she grumbled, hearing the whine in her voice. Her friends would be all over them when they got back to the castle, and then dinner…

"Who says you have to wait?" Flynn's fingers grew more insistent.

She moaned softly. "What?"

"We're the only ones on this flight, if you hadn't noticed," he murmured as his hand slid beneath her skirt. "But tell me if this makes you uncomfortable."

She glanced around the interior of the Langdon jet, taking in the empty leather seats, the bar to their left, the partition separating them from the cockpit. There was no flight attendant, as they had access to a variety of refreshments in the bar. Flynn was right. They were, for all intents and purposes, alone. "It doesn't."

He pushed aside her panties, bringing his fingers against her bare skin.

"Oh my God." Her voice had gone impossibly high pitched.

Flynn rested his forehead against hers, leaning in close as his fingers began to work. His thumb circled her clit as he pressed two fingers against her opening, teasing her, testing her. She whimpered, spreading her legs wider to encourage him, and he took full advantage. His fingers stroked and plunged, giving pressure and friction everywhere she needed it.

"Yes," she whispered. "More. Please."

"Anything," he answered, capturing her mouth as he stroked harder, faster, and her whole body convulsed in the seat. She ground herself against his hand, and then she was flying...literally and figuratively. The orgasm ripped through her, fast and fierce, leaving her panting and dazzled.

She grinned, eyes closed as aftershocks of pleasure drifted through her like the fluffy white clouds below. "Does this mean I just joined the mile-high club?"

His eyes crinkled in a wide smile. "I'd say it does, love."

"Talk about ending my trip with a bang."

13

---

*R*uby felt slightly off-balance as she walked down the steps from the Langdon jet and crossed the tarmac to the car waiting for them. James, Rosemont Castle's driver, tipped his hat to her with a warm smile.

"Welcome home, Miss Ruby."

"Thanks, James. It's good to be home."

"And a pleasure to meet you, Mr. Bowen," he said to Flynn, shaking his hand before loading their luggage into the trunk of the Bentley.

"Very nice to meet you too." Flynn opened the door for her and motioned her inside.

She'd sat in this car dozens of times, hundreds maybe. It felt familiar, comforting. And yet different somehow, with Flynn sitting beside her. Two worlds colliding, her real life with her fantasy vacation. It was just past three here in Virginia, but to her body clock, it was after nine, and she was absolutely wiped from the trip.

She rested her head against the glass as James drove them to the castle, watching the Appalachian Mountains unfurl outside the window, dotted now with liberal amounts of red and gold. Fall had officially arrived here at home while she was playing house with a fancy Brit in Paris. "Beautiful, isn't it?"

Flynn stared out of his own window, seemingly fascinated with the scenery. "It is. I've never seen anything quite like it before."

"We don't really get foliage like this in Florida either, or maybe it's just that we don't have mountains like these. This is only my second fall in Virginia, but I think I'm in love. It might even replace spring as my favorite season."

"I can certainly see why." He looked over at her. "You look exhausted."

"I may need a nap before dinner."

"That sounds like an excellent idea."

She couldn't shake that weird, off-balance feeling as the Bentley drove down Rosemont Castle's winding drive. She was home. Everything looked exactly as it had when she left—except the foliage—but she felt different. No, that wasn't quite true either. She was the same person she'd been when she left, but her solo adventure across Europe had become so much bigger and longer and more meaningful than she'd ever expected.

She'd seen and done and experienced things that would forever color her worldview. And she'd brought one of those things home with her. Flynn looked at ease next to her, taking his first look at Rosemont Castle a lot more calmly than most, but then again, he'd grown up amongst castles and estates and all sorts of grandeur in England.

"It's really something, isn't it?" he commented as the Bentley pulled up in front of the guest house where Ruby lived now. "Looks like a bit of classic England right here in America."

"Probably the only one like it," she agreed. "Oh geez."

Elle and Megan were sprinting across the lawn in their direction. Flynn chuckled as he got out of the car. "Eager to see you, aren't they?"

"Just a bit." But Ruby was awfully glad to see them too. In

fact, as she stood, she couldn't contain the huge grin that had overtaken her face.

Megan and Elle swooped in, grabbing her in a group hug so enthusiastic that both of her feet actually left the ground for a second. "Boy, are we glad to see you," Elle said, one arm wrapped securely around Ruby's waist as she made sure she had her footing.

"It's good to see you guys too. Really good." She squeezed them back, as her throat tightened and her vision blurred. These women had been her best friends since they were kids, the kind of friendship that lasted a lifetime. They'd been by her side through just about every illness she'd ever had. When she'd been too sick to have visitors, they'd sat outside her bedroom window and passed her notes to keep her up on all the gossip from school.

And she'd missed them. A lot.

"Hi, Flynn," Megan said as she disentangled herself from their hug to shake his hand. "I hear we owe you a huge thanks for taking such good care of Ruby for us."

"It was my pleasure," he said, seeming somehow even more British now that he stood on American soil.

"We were probably introduced at the wedding," Elle said, extending a hand. "But honestly, I met so many people that night, it's kind of a blur. I'm Elle."

"A pleasure," he said as he took her hand and shook.

"I can't wait to catch up with you guys and hear all about your honeymoon, Elle, but jetlag is a bitch. Flynn and I are going to take a nap before dinner," Ruby told them.

"Absolutely," Elle said, her blue eyes crinkled in concern. "You should sleep. We'll contain our excitement and nosiness about your trip until you're rested."

"What she said." Megan linked her arm in Elle's, and they started back toward the castle. "See you guys in a little while. And welcome home."

"They're very excited to see you," Flynn commented with an amused twinkle in his eye as she unlocked her front door.

"We're like family at this point." She pushed the door open and stepped inside, tugging her suitcase behind her. "We all lived in guest rooms at the main castle when we first got here. But after Elle moved into the owner's quarters with Theo, and Megan moved into the farmhouse with Jake, I came down here to the guest house. Feels much homier."

"It's nice," Flynn said as he moved the rest of their bags over the threshold.

Ruby clucked her tongue, eager for this next reunion too. "Simon? Oliver? I hope you guys haven't forgotten me."

Simon's gray head poked around the doorway from the bedroom, and he trotted down the hall toward her, meowing all the way. As she turned to greet him, she saw Oliver sprawled on the couch in the living room, eyeing her balefully as if deciding whether he still loved her after she'd left him for three weeks.

"I missed you guys." She squatted down and scooped Simon into her arms. He pressed his head against her cheek, purring loudly and still meowing his happiness to see her.

"He's a talkative one," Flynn commented, crouching beside her.

"They're Siamese. They tend to be that way."

Simon leaned out of her arms to sniff Flynn's extended hand before nuzzling him. Oliver hopped off the couch and strolled over, stalking around Flynn with his tail held high.

"Didn't want to be left out, hm?" She reached out to pet him, and he rubbed against her thigh, purring even louder than his brother before making his way over to Flynn.

"Well, I guess I've passed muster," Flynn said, laughter in his tone, as both cats circled him, demanding his attention.

"You have," she agreed, standing.

Together, they moved their luggage to the master bedroom, where Flynn insisted they take a quick shower before bed to wash off any germs she might have accumulated during their travels, despite the private jet. Always so considerate.

The hot shower refreshed her, but somehow made her even more tired. As she slipped into her bed with Flynn beside her, she finally realized the difference between pre and post-trip Ruby. She'd left this house a single woman in search of adventure, and she'd returned a woman in love.

~

FLYNN WOKE TO THE SENSATION OF BEING POKED IN THE crotch. What the hell? He reached out reflexively, his hands encountering fur. One of Ruby's cats sat on top of him with a paw pressing into his balls. Careful not to startle him and engage the claws, Flynn lifted the cat and set him on the floor. That's when he saw the other cat stretched out on Ruby's chest, fast asleep. Apparently, they were glad to have her home.

A quick glance at the clock told him it was just past five. Jetlag really was a bitch, because he was simultaneously restless and exhausted. Outside the window, the sun was just dipping below the treetops as afternoon turned to evening. They were due up at the main castle for dinner soon, but Ruby looked so peaceful, he couldn't bring himself to wake her. No doubt, she needed the sleep.

He slipped out of bed and padded down the hall to the kitchen for a glass of water. The cat that had awoken him followed, darting in and out between his feet as he walked. "Are you Simon or Oliver?" Flynn asked the cat. They looked very similar, with light gray bodies, darker gray on their heads and paws, and striking blue eyes. Siamese, Ruby had said.

"Meow," the cat answered, jumping up on the counter to watch as Flynn filled a glass with water from the spout on the refrigerator.

"You guys take good care of her, don't you?" He drank it down without pausing for breath.

The cat never took its eyes off him. "Meow."

Flynn set his glass in the sink and moved to the window, staring up at the castle. Somehow, he couldn't quite imagine Ruby living there. The Ruby he knew was too practical and sensible to live in an overdone mansion of a home like Rosemont Castle. The guest house suited her, though.

"See that tower on the left-hand side of the castle?" she said softly from behind him.

He turned. "I didn't hear you get up."

She wrapped her arms around his waist. "That was my bedroom."

"What was?"

"The top of the tower."

He looked at the tower, with its semi-circular walls and oversized windows. "Really?"

"Remember how I told you that we all lived in guest rooms at the castle when we first got here? That was mine."

"Very Rapunzel of you," he said, reaching around playfully to tug at her hair.

"It did have sort of a fairytale princess vibe," she told him. "And the views were amazing. But I like living here in the guest house a lot more. That room felt like a fun vacation, but this feels like home."

"I can see that."

"Time to get ready for dinner." She leaned in to press a kiss against his cheek.

"Are you feeling up for it?" He'd heard her cough a few times since they landed in Virginia, and he couldn't shake the feeling she needed sleep more than she needed to socialize with her friends tonight.

"I'm exhausted, so we won't stay too long, but I'm also starving. Besides, if we go back to sleep now, we'll be awake in the middle of the night, ready to start the day."

"That's true." The best way to acclimate to jetlag was to go to bed at the right time in your new time zone. He followed her to the bedroom to get dressed. Ruby put on snug-fitting jeans and a flowy orange top, and he couldn't resist pulling her in for a lengthy kiss before they started their walk up to the castle. "I love that color on you."

"Thank you." She slid her hand into his and squeezed.

Outside, it was cool and crisp, refreshing against his gritty, tired eyes. "So much quieter than London."

"The only thing you hear outside at night are the bugs singing. I love it. It's so different here from where I grew up. Feels so good to breathe in all that fresh air." She sucked in a long, audible breath, coughing on the exhale.

"Should I worry about that cough?" he asked cautiously.

She shook her head. "I'll be coughing off and on for weeks after a bout of pneumonia like that, but the dry air on the airplane probably aggravated it a bit."

"That makes sense." They walked up the stone steps to the castle's front door, and he pulled it open, stepping back to motion her inside. "After you, my lady."

"Why thank you." She gave him a devilish grin.

They followed the sound of voices toward the kitchen, where Elle, Theo, Megan, and Jake were gathered with glasses of wine, talking and laughing. Ruby tugged Flynn's fingers, her excitement palpable as she led him toward her friends. There was more hugging, and back slaps for Flynn from both Theo and Jake. An older woman with graying hair pulled Ruby into a tight embrace, exclaiming how worried she'd been.

"Thanks, Beatrice," Ruby told her with an affectionate smile. "This is Flynn Bowen. He and Theo went to school together."

"Oh, I've heard all about your adventures with Flynn these past few weeks," Beatrice said, turning to Flynn with arms extended. "It's so nice to meet you. I've cooked for the Langdons for over thirty years."

"A pleasure," he told her as she enveloped him in a warm hug, catching him slightly off guard. Obviously, things were more casual here in America than they were in Great Britain. He wasn't sure he'd ever hugged his own cook, but he couldn't help but be taken by the warm, family-like atmosphere in Theo's kitchen.

More wine was poured, and they migrated into the dining room for salads and bread before their meal, while Elle and Megan peppered Ruby for details about her time in Paris.

"Not quite the adventure I had planned," she said, darting a glance over at Flynn. "I'll admit, it was intimidating getting sick in a foreign country where I didn't speak the language while I was traveling alone."

"Wouldn't have known it by the way you tried to keep me from coming to stay with you," he said, nudging her elbow with his.

"I'm known to be a bit stubborn," she said with a shrug and a smile.

"She's a lot stubborn," Megan confirmed. "I would have been on the next flight to Paris if you hadn't convinced her to let you stay."

"I had a feeling that might be the case." He'd gotten a glimpse at the strength of their friendship that morning they'd had breakfast together in London. "But it made more sense for it to be me. I was so much closer and able to work remotely."

"Oh, I think it turned out perfectly," Megan said with a sly smile.

"Megan!" Ruby shot her an embarrassed look.

He squeezed her knee beneath the table. "I was glad I could help."

"So were we," Elle said diplomatically. "It gave us all peace of mind knowing you were there with her. Otherwise, I would have spent my whole honeymoon worrying."

"Speaking of your honeymoon, I need details," Ruby said. "And pictures."

And so, conversation shifted to Elle and Theo's honeymoon in Tahiti. They regaled the table with stories about their vacation. Ruby ended up on the other side of the table with one arm around Elle's shoulders as she looked at photos on her phone.

They ate chicken Florentine and shared more casual, comfortable conversation than Flynn could remember sharing with a group of friends in ages. The truth was, he spent most of his time traveling to work locations, supervising crew, or conducting business with various corporate associates. Even family dinners tended to focus on talk about Exeter.

By the time he and Ruby left the castle, he was comfortably full and relaxed, eyes watery from so much laughter. "Your friends are fantastic."

Ruby looked over at him with a smile. "They're the best."

"I have to agree." It drove a dagger through his chest because he knew, after tonight, he could never ask her to leave Rosemont Castle for him. But it also gave him peace about heading out tomorrow, because he could always picture her here, happy and thriving, surrounded by people who loved her. Ruby was a gem in every sense of the word.

"I'm glad you're here," she said.

"I am too. And I'm glad I'll get to see a little more of the area with you tomorrow before I leave. But right now, I'm glad to spend this night with you."

"I'm pretty happy about that too." She gave him a look that set his blood pumping.

He was more than happy that he'd gotten to spend those two weeks with her while she was recuperating, but now that she was well, and especially after that moment they'd shared together on the plane, he wanted—*needed*—this last night with her.

If she was up for it.

"You must be tired," he said.

"Not that tired." She stopped and turned, claiming his mouth for a kiss that lit every cell in his body on fire.

"I'm really glad to hear that." He slid his palms down her

back, pressing her closer, lost in the feel of her breasts against his chest, the roll of her hips as they met his.

"Look up," she whispered.

He did and found himself staring into an endless expanse of stars overhead, highlighted by the moon, which hung bright and round just above the tree line to their left. "Full moon."

"Mm hmm. Sounds like a good excuse for anything and everything we want to do tonight." She slid her fingers through his belt loop and yanked, leading him toward the guest house.

And he sure as hell wasn't going to argue with that. He followed, hands roaming wherever he could reach as they walked. She let them into the guest house, locking the door behind them. "Alone at last."

"My three favorite words," he murmured, pushing her up against the wall.

A funny look flashed through her eyes, but it was gone almost before he could even wonder what it had been. And then they were kissing, and all the lust he'd pushed aside while she was sick came rushing to the surface. His cock hardened, pushing against the fabric of his trousers, aching in time to the pounding of his heart.

"Been waiting all night to do this." She jumped up, wrapping her legs around his hips. "Take me to bed."

14

*R*uby woke, simultaneously disoriented and relieved to find herself in Virginia. Her bed. Her house. All the familiar sights and smells of home, including a warm cat curled over her feet.

And Flynn sprawled across the sheets beside her.

Not hers. Not familiar, at least not in the context of home. And yet, waking beside him had come to be as familiar as waking with a cat on her feet. It felt good and right. They'd left "one day in London" status behind ages ago. Maybe they'd never really achieved it, because the feelings had always been there, rooted in the instant connection that had bound them together since they met at Elle's wedding.

He'd be leaving after lunch, headed to DC for a business meeting. Pre-trip Ruby would have pushed her feelings to the side and said goodbye as planned. But as she rolled toward him in bed, her bare chest pressed against his, bodies warm and sluggish with sleep, she knew she didn't want to say goodbye. She wanted a relationship with Flynn, whatever it might look like, no matter how risky or dangerous or uncharted.

Hadn't that been the whole point of her adventure? If she

was going to *really* embrace this new side of herself, she had to throw caution to the wind and go after what she wanted. And that meant, she couldn't let Flynn leave Virginia without telling him how she felt.

"Morning," he said, wrapping an arm around her.

"Good morning."

"Did you sleep well?" he asked as his hand roamed upward into the tangled depths of her hair.

"So well I don't remember a moment of it."

"The best kind of sleep," he said.

"Especially when I have you beside me."

"Especially then." He brought his hips into alignment with hers so she could feel his hard cock pressing against her.

"Hold that thought," she whispered before sliding out of bed. She went into the bathroom to pee, brushing her teeth for good measure while she was in there, before climbing back into bed.

Flynn lay just where she'd left him, sheets tangled around his legs, cock still standing at attention. She crawled across the bed to straddle him, letting his cock rest between her thighs.

"Love waking up this way," she said, rocking her hips against his.

"Agreed." His fingers dug into her ass, sliding her up and down the length of his cock, igniting a fire inside her, concentrated in her clit, which throbbed at the contact.

She dipped her head and kissed him, nipping at his lower lip as their bodies moved together, letting the heat and the friction between them build. That was the best thing about morning sex, in her opinion. Everything was relaxed and unhurried, softened by the last remnants of sleep lingering in her veins.

They kissed as the sun crested the treetops outside, touching and teasing in its gentle light. Eventually, Flynn reached for a condom on the bedside table and rolled it on. She sank onto him, leaning forward so that her breasts brushed against his chest, creating a delicious friction as their bodies moved together.

This was another thing that came with time, knowing just how her body fit with his, what his lips tasted like first thing in the morning—the sharp spearmint of his toothpaste—and how the brown of his eyes seemed almost green in the morning light, a mossy color that sucked her in, locking her in his gaze as it liquefied the closer he grew to his release.

She rocked her hips faster, using the leverage of her position to grind her clit against him as she moved, and with a gasp, release rushed through her. Flynn thrust into her hard and fast, tensing with a groan as he came inside her.

She rolled onto the sheets beside him, snuggling her face against his chest as her heart rate returned to normal. "Now I'm awake."

"Me too." His fingers combed gently through her hair.

"Elle insisted on sending breakfast down to us this morning, so we can stay in bed as long as we like."

"Brilliant."

In the end, they snuggled in bed until their breakfast platter arrived, and then they ate apple-cinnamon French toast, poached eggs, and fresh fruit at the little table in the kitchen. She wore a green knit robe, and he wore only his boxer briefs.

She'd never lived with anyone the way she'd lived with Flynn these last few weeks. Probably, she would have thought she wasn't ready for that kind of step, that she'd miss her freedom and independence, but she didn't feel like she was missing either of those things when they were together. She just enjoyed being with him.

After breakfast, they showered and dressed. "Feel like going for a walk around the grounds?" she asked.

"I'd love to."

So, they put on jackets and left the guest house. Outside, the October morning was cool and brisk, dew gleaming on the grass so that it seemed to sparkle in the sunshine. The sky was a perfect shade of blue, offsetting the gray of the castle walls. The flower beds around the fountain in front had been filled with mums in fall hues, purple, burgundy, and a deep orange, a more vivid version of the treetops in the distance.

"Let's go this way first." She led Flynn away from the castle, toward the pastures where several horses grazed and the walking trails beyond. "Jake rents the barn. He trains horses for a living. That's his horse, Twister." She pointed to a beautiful red-coated horse in the nearest pasture. Twister raised his head and whinnied, trotting over to the fence to greet them. "And the funny-looking little white mare in there with him is Bug. She came to us as a rescue horse in our Fairy Tails program, but Jake adopted her for Megan."

Bug trotted over behind Twister, ears pricked and tail swooshing as she sized Flynn up. Her white coat was dappled with darker spots, her face and neck marred by dull pink scars from a dog attack before she arrived at Rosemont Castle.

Ruby walked to the fence. She stroked Twister's face as he stood happily munching on a mouthful of grass. Beside her, Flynn reached out to rub Twister's neck.

"I can see why you like it here so much," he said.

"It's so outrageous, but so perfect at the same time." She took his hand, leading the way toward one of the many hiking trails that crisscrossed the property. "Good to be home, where I don't have to wear a mask to go outside." The air here on the castle grounds was about as clean as she could hope to find, a world away from downtown Paris. As beautiful as it was, a city was a city, as far as air quality was concerned.

Conversation was sparse as they walked, but it felt comfortable, a silence that didn't need to be filled. In the distance, a car passed on the drive headed up to the castle. A dog barked. An airplane zoomed across the blue sky, leaving a white trail in its wake. The sights and sounds of home.

As they entered the woods, she took Flynn's hand in hers.

Dry leaves crunched beneath their feet, with the accompanying scent of the forest, slightly musty but not in an unpleasant way. Overhead, the trees provided a canopy of leaves, various shades of green, yellow, orange, red, and brown, a fall kaleidoscope of color.

"I love coming out here for walks," she said. "Elle goes jogging on these trails. Jake rides his horse. Megan brings her camera and takes pictures. I just like to walk and soak it all in."

"And I'm picturing how I'd landscape that hilltop over there to put in a rustic little cabin, tucked away here in the forest." Flynn gave her hand a squeeze, his eyes dancing with inspiration as he looked around.

"You have the eye of an architect, all right," she said. "Will you check in with Aidan again before you fly to Dubai?"

He nodded. "As soon as I'm back in the UK."

"I'd love to see it when it's finished. You know, a picture or whatever." She glanced over at him.

"I'll send you one."

They kept walking, meandering their way along the trail. Her impulse was to rush ahead, but her lungs weren't fully healed yet, so she had to take her time. She stopped here and there to sip water and kiss Flynn, enjoying their last morning together. Or not, if she had any say in it. Because she didn't want this to be their last morning together.

Finally, even moving at a post-pneumonia snail's pace, they came out at the overlook. It was a spot on the trail where the forest opened, revealing the castle and grounds below. After she, Megan, and Elle had discovered it, they'd had a bench carved out of a nearby fallen tree so guests could sit here with a bottle of wine and enjoy the view.

If only she'd thought to bring a bottle of wine with her and Flynn...although it was a bit early in the day for that. Mimosas, though. Oh well, hindsight and everything.

She tugged his hand, and they sat together on the bench. "Pretty, isn't it?"

"This is what they call a million-dollar view," he said.

"It is," she agreed.

"Now, I'll be able to picture you here, and in your guest house, and up at the main castle. I'm glad for the chance to know where you call home." There was something wistful in his tone, and it only strengthened her resolve to do what she was about to do.

"Home can be anywhere you make it, though," she said, turning on the bench to face him. "I spent a lot of my life confined to my house, and now that I've finally gotten the chance to spread my wings, I've realized how much more there is in the world."

"I agree with that." He studied her, no doubt wondering at the urgency in her voice. "I spend most of my life traveling, although I suppose London will always feel like home."

"I don't want to say goodbye, Flynn."

He sat up straighter on the bench. "Ruby—"

"No, let me say what I need to say." She reached for his hand and gave it a squeeze. "One thing I've learned is that life can be short and fragile, and when you find something great, you should grab ahold of it, even if it's not what you were expecting. And I definitely wasn't expecting you, but here we are."

"I wasn't expecting you either." Something in his expression softened.

She took a deep breath and looked him straight in the eye. "So, if you feel the same way, I'd really like to give this thing between us a chance. I don't care what it looks like or if it involves a lot of long-distance dating or if we don't see each other much while you're in Dubai. I just think we should give it a try and see if it could work. Because...I think I'm falling in love with you."

Flynn lurched off the bench, pacing to the edge of the

overlook. Behind him, Ruby was quiet, but he felt her stare like a prickle at the back of his neck. "I...I'm sorry. I'm not quite sure how to respond."

"You don't have to say anything. I just wanted you to know how I feel before you leave," she said. "And if you have any feelings for me at all, if you feel sad about the idea of saying goodbye, then maybe we could just agree to keep our options open? Let's stay in touch and see what happens."

"I do have feelings for you, Ruby." He turned to face her. "I hope you know that. I've enjoyed these last few weeks with you more than I can remember enjoying anything in recent years. Under other circumstances, I would love nothing more than to continue our relationship. But the reality is that your life is here at Rosemont Castle, and mine is in Dubai, and then wherever the company sends me next."

"So, we try things long-distance for a while and see what happens," she said, undeterred.

"I wish I could say yes." He wanted to more than anything, but he knew in the long run, he'd only be prolonging the inevitable. His lifestyle wasn't suited for a stable relationship. He was always on the go, always jetting off to the next location. It was the only thing that even came close to keeping him satisfied. What could he really offer Ruby other than frustration and heartbreak? He couldn't bear to watch it happen, couldn't bear to hurt her. He wouldn't be the man who took her away from her family and friends here in America, from the life she'd built for herself at Rosemont Castle.

He walked back over to sit beside her. "You deserve a man who can give you everything, who can build a life with you here in Virginia."

"Don't tell me what I deserve," she said, no longer quite meeting his eyes. "I'll be the judge of that."

He stared over the golden-hued treetops at the castle in the distance. "You're right," he agreed. "But I know that, right now,

I'm not in a position to offer enough of myself to meet my own standards for what a relationship should be. And it would kill me to disappoint you."

"So, you think it's better not to even try?" Ruby stood abruptly from the bench and marched down the path toward the castle, head held high, arms wrapped around herself.

"I'm sorry," he called after her as a sense of heaviness came over him, weighing down his steps as he started down the trail behind her. All the beauty and charm seemed to have been sucked out of the morning. Now, the air felt cold, trees swaying harshly overhead as dead brown leaves swirled through the air around him.

Ruby didn't say another word as she tromped down the path, not even when he fell into step beside her. They walked in silence, not the easy, comfortable silence they'd shared from time to time on the way up, but a harsh, ringing silence that reinforced how much he'd lost with every crunch of his shoe against the leafy trail bed.

They left the forest a lot more quickly than they'd entered it, coming back onto the castle grounds behind the horse pastures. Ruby led the way back to the guest house, but when they walked inside, she tossed her jacket over a chair in the kitchen and headed down the hall toward the bedroom.

"I'm going to rest for a little while before lunch," she told him, closing the door behind her.

Flynn stood in the living room, feeling more inadequate than he'd ever felt in his life. Not knowing what else to do, he sat at the kitchen table with his laptop and spent the next hour going back and forth with the builders for Aidan's property, answering questions and tweaking final details. All the while, a sick feeling churned in the pit of his stomach, like he'd just gone for the bottom step and missed and now he was hanging in mid-air, waiting to fall.

Promptly at noon, Ruby emerged from the bedroom,

looking refreshed and calm. "Time to head up to the castle for your farewell lunch." Both cats trailed her down the hall, giving Flynn condescending looks, as if they knew and judged him for everything that had happened. He closed his laptop and put it away, grabbing his jacket as he followed her out the door.

Ruby was polite, if distant, as they walked to the castle to join her friends for lunch. Soon, they were enveloped in conversation that hid any awkwardness between them. Flynn told them all about the project he'd been working on for Aidan and his upcoming work in Dubai. Theo, in particular, had a lot of questions, as his family and Flynn's had done business together for generations. Langdon Fine Furnishings and Exeter Hotels went way back.

"Don't you ever get tired of all the travel?" Megan asked, eyes darting between him and Ruby.

"Not really, no. It keeps things interesting," he told her.

Ruby stared at her plate like it was a to-do list for the rest of her life.

"I do find it tiresome at times," Theo chimed in, "splitting my time between here and London. Mostly, though, it's all gone much more smoothly than I'd anticipated." He reached over and covered Elle's hand with his.

Flynn glanced at Ruby. She was stabbing at her salad like it had personally offended her. Her expression betrayed nothing, but she was uncharacteristically quiet, which seemed somehow harder to take than if she'd just started yelling at him.

After lunch had been cleared away, he said his goodbyes to Megan, Jake, Elle, and Theo. He noticed that Ruby lingered in the castle, showing him this and that, so that they ended up walking down to the guest house only a few minutes before his car was scheduled to arrive. Back in her house, she watched quietly as he repacked the few items he'd taken out of his bag. He set it by the door, shooing away the cat that ran over to try to stuff himself inside.

Outside, he heard tires crunching over gravel.

He turned to face Ruby. "I guess this is it, then."

"I guess so." She met his gaze for the first time since their argument in the woods, her eyes intense and defiant, daring him to get through this goodbye without making things between them even worse.

"I'll miss you, more than you'll probably ever know." He took her hands, asking silently for one last hug, one last kiss. It was probably more than he deserved, but she gave it to him anyway. With a sigh, she stepped into his embrace, clasping her hands behind his neck.

"I'll miss you too," she whispered, her eyes gone suspiciously glossy.

He lowered his head, pressing his lips against hers. She sucked his bottom lip into her mouth, biting down as she turned the kiss from gentle to ferocious in the span of a heartbeat. They groped at each other, tongues tangling, emotions manifesting in the heat between them. He slid a hand into her hair and tugged, loosening the ever-present knot at the back of her head.

A knock at the door drove them apart.

Ruby stepped out of his arms, cheeks flushed, eyes snapping with heat and hurt. She licked her lips, crossing her arms over her chest as she looked out the window at the driver waiting to take him away. "I guess this is goodbye, then."

He took a deep breath to calm his heart before he went outside. "Goodbye, Ruby."

Afraid of what he might say—or do—if he lingered, he picked up his duffel bag and briefcase and headed for the door. As he slid into the backseat of the car waiting in the driveway, he ignored the ache in his chest. In the end, this would hurt less than watching their relationship disintegrate across oceans and continents.

He was sure of it.

The car backed up to turn around, and he found himself meeting Ruby's eyes as she watched him out the kitchen window. And then, he was moving down the driveway, on his way toward DC and Wales and Dubai and wherever life might carry him next.

15

*H*er list was getting out of control. Ruby drummed her fingers against the keyboard of her laptop. Behind her, late afternoon sun filtered through the window, warming her back. Simon lay on the table beside her laptop, while Oliver had curled himself over her feet. They were glad to have her home and had hardly left her side, especially since Flynn left.

She sucked in a breath, determined not to spend any more time crying over everything that had happened that morning. Yes, she'd cried about it. But now, she was attempting to be productive, because after three weeks in Europe without her laptop, there was a *lot* to catch up on. At this point, she had a list to keep track of all her lists.

And, since there was no time like the present, she pulled up the interface for the castle's website and began tackling the updates that needed to be made. She added a blog post about Elle and Theo's wedding with a few of their professional wedding photos, since they were the owners of Rosemont Castle. Megan had sent her some new fall photos of the castle and grounds to add to their online gallery, and the adoptable animals in their Fairy Tails program all needed updates.

The next thing she knew, someone was knocking on her front door. Not *someone*. She knew that knock as well as she knew her own, and a reluctant smile crossed her face as she stood from the table and stretched, feeling a satisfying pop somewhere in the base of her spine. Tomorrow, she needed to get back to her office in the castle, because working at the kitchen table was not the most comfortable thing.

Sure enough, Elle and Megan stood outside the door, each carrying a silver tray from the castle. Ruby's stomach grumbled at the sight, because, wow yeah, it was past six already. She opened the door, motioning them in. "Miss me already?"

"We thought you might need some company tonight," Elle said as she set her tray on the table and pulled a bottle of red wine out of the bag that had been slung over her shoulder.

"And we missed you," Megan added with a grin.

"Plus, we want all the unabridged details of your trip, now that it's girls' ears only." Elle winked as she moved to the cabinet and took out three wineglasses.

"I'm glad you guys are here," Ruby admitted. This was exactly what she needed tonight. She pulled open a drawer in the island and took out the corkscrew, setting to work on the bottle of wine. "I could use a good chat-fest tonight."

"And a sob-fest too, if you need one." Elle placed a hand on her shoulder with a sympathetic smile. "How did it go when you and Flynn said goodbye? I thought I picked up on some weird vibes between you guys at lunchtime."

"Oh, there were weird vibes, all right." Ruby poured herself a glass of wine and took a fortifying sip. She waited until they'd all filled their plates and settled themselves on the oversized couch in the living room before she told them what had gone down during her hike with Flynn that morning.

"Holy shit, you told him you were falling in love with him?" Megan exclaimed.

Elle set her plate on the table and pulled Ruby in for a hug. "I'm so sorry, sweetie."

"It's okay, you guys. I'm feeling pretty heartbroken about it, but I don't know, maybe he was right to end things now instead of trying to make it work long distance."

Elle scoffed. "Love is always worth fighting for. Just look at Theo and me. Things seemed so hopeless for us at first too, but we made it work, and splitting our time between here and London hasn't even been that big of a deal. It's been fun."

"Yeah, but Flynn doesn't just work in London. He travels to job sites all over the world. How would I have a life if I was always following him around, living out of a suitcase while he oversees new hotels being built?"

"Well, how did you envision it when you asked him for the chance?" Megan asked.

Ruby spiraled a bite of pasta around her fork as she pondered her answer. "I guess...I guess I really didn't. I just knew how I felt, and how *right* it felt when we were living together in Paris, and I just wanted to fight for any chance to make things work."

"Well, for what it's worth, I think you were one hundred percent right to fight for that chance," Elle said. "I mean, how would you know if it would work until you tried?"

"Maybe he'll get home and realize you were right," Megan offered before stuffing a bite of bread into her mouth.

Ruby was already shaking her head before she'd formulated her response. "I don't think so. He seemed pretty firm on it. And it's not just the traveling. He's been under a lot of scrutiny from his family. They've always treated him like somewhat of a screw-up, and I think he's taken it to heart." She sighed into her wine. "So, I think that's probably affecting his judgment too."

Elle frowned behind her wineglass. "A screw-up, how?"

"He struggled a lot in school before he was diagnosed with ADHD, and he's struggled to find a spot in the family business that really suits him too." She paused, staring into the depths of her wine. "If you ask me, he doesn't belong in the hotel business at all. He's an architect at heart, and he does amazing work. He should open his own firm and build things that excite him. He could still collaborate with Exeter if he wanted. But he's afraid of letting them down again, so I think he'll just stay, doing something he doesn't really love to make them happy."

"Well, that's sad," Megan said.

"It is," Ruby agreed. "But he has to make those decisions for himself. And while I'm kind of crushed right now, I'll be okay. I have you guys to help me get back on my feet." She smiled as they embraced her for a group hug.

"Always," Elle said fiercely. "We will always be here for each other."

After dinner, they opened a second bottle of wine, put on a cheesy movie, and made a proper girls' night out of it. By the time they left, Ruby was feeling much better. When she got in bed that night, she mentally ran through her to-do list for the next day. It was good to be home and get back into all her routines. Good. Definitely good.

As if they had a mind of their own, her fingers opened the camera roll on her phone, scrolling through the pictures of her time in London and Paris with Flynn. Before she knew it, tears were streaming down her cheeks. They looked so happy together. They'd shared so many laughs, such an easy rapport. Ruby didn't often open her heart to people. She usually analyzed every decision before she leaped. She'd been different with Flynn, more uninhibited.

And she meant to hang onto that newly discovered part of herself, even if it meant letting go of Flynn in the process.

∼

MISERY.

That's what Flynn's first day back in London felt like. He spent the majority of the day in meetings, fighting the constant urge to tap his pen obnoxiously against the table or shuffle his feet against the carpet. How could they spend so many hours talking about a building that would wind up looking like every other hotel they'd built?

He stared at the screen in the front of the room, looking at the final rendering for the hotel in Dubai. It was tall and sleek, with the trademark Exeter logo near the top. A striking building, no doubt. It would attract plenty of business once it was complete, another jewel in the Exeter crown. And he couldn't muster even the slightest bit of excitement about overseeing its construction.

His chest physically ached at the thought of spending the next six months doing just that. In his mind's eye, he saw himself sitting in the flat in Paris with Ruby. He'd felt more relaxed in his weeks there than he could ever remember feeling. Happy. Inspired, as he worked on the design for Aidan's house. The relentless restlessness that was his constant companion at Exeter had been absent in those weeks.

The meeting broke up, and he made for the door, eager to step outside for some fresh air to clear his head.

"Flynn." His mother's voice halted him in his tracks.

He turned to face her. "Mother."

"It's so good to have you in the office this week," she said with a warm smile. "We do miss seeing you when you're off working on job sites. How did everything turn out with your friend in Paris?"

"She's fully recovered and back home in the states," he told her.

"I'm glad to hear it." She rested a hand on his arm, her eyes searching his. "You're a good friend to look after her like that."

"I was glad I was able to help."

"And is she just a friend?" his mother asked, finally coming around to the question that had no doubt been at the forefront of her mind since he'd gone to stay with Ruby in Paris.

"She was more than a friend, but that's all she is now, all she can be, given the ocean between us." He shoved his hands into the front pockets of his trousers, fighting the urge to fidget in front of her.

"Walk with me," she said, turning toward the door that led outside, as if she'd sensed his discomfort. "You know how much your father and I have wanted to see you settle down," she said as she pushed open the door and led the way onto the street. Exeter's headquarters were located on bustling Coleman Street, but this side door led onto a quiet back alley where they could walk and talk more easily.

"I know," he answered her. "I suppose I will someday."

"We could find a different place for you in the company." Her heels clicked on the pavement as they walked, punctuating her words.

"What?"

"So you could stay here in London. That's what's stopping you, isn't it? The fact that you're always traveling around the world?"

"It's one thing," he answered carefully. He'd tried out virtually every desk job there was here at headquarters. None of them had suited him then, and they wouldn't suit him now.

She looked up at him. "This girl in Paris seems different from your previous relationships. There's something in your voice when you talk about her. You seem to like her quite a lot, and I don't want you to throw it away because you think you can't settle down."

He kept walking, lips pressed tightly together. What did he say to that? The thought of spending weeks, months, *years* here at headquarters made him want to scream. It would ruin him, and what good would he be to Ruby then? "It's something to consider," he said finally.

"Good, then." She nodded briskly, as if it was a done deal. "We need you in Dubai, but I can arrange for you to stay here in London thereafter if you wish. Just say the word."

"I'll let you know."

They'd circled around the block and entered the building through its flashy front doors on Coleman Street. Walking in circles. The story of his life.

16

Flynn stepped out of his car and walked toward the home site in progress. Trees had been cut to accommodate the house and a small yard, leaving most of the canopy overhead intact to preserve the look and view.

"Off to a good start, aren't we?" Aidan walked toward him from the other side of the clearing.

"Yes," Flynn agreed. Now that he could see the beginnings of the construction, he knew they'd made the right decisions as to the location and positioning of the house. The Wye River twinkled below, a view that just wouldn't quit.

"Knew you were the right man for the job." Aidan clapped him on the back. They walked together toward the edge of the property, looking out over the valley beyond.

It reminded Flynn of the lookout on the trail at Rosemont Castle, the conversation he'd had with Ruby there, all the ways his life seemed to have run off track since he'd left her behind. Standing here with Aidan, he felt the first flickering of peace since that moment. Maybe it was the outdoors, the view, the company.

Maybe it was that he wasn't at Exeter.

"I showed the final renderings to a friend of mine," Aidan said. "He was impressed."

"Is that so?" Flynn kept his eyes on the valley below.

"He's looking to build," Aidan went on. "He invited you to submit a bid if you're interested."

"Hmm." Was he interested? Was this what he wanted, to work full time as an architect and leave Exeter behind? Would that solve anything for him, or would he just travel the globe in a different capacity?

"You should do it."

"I'll think about it," Flynn told him. "How soon does he want to build? Because I'm committed in Dubai for the next six months."

"I know you are, mate, and I told him that. He's not looking to build until next year."

Flynn dragged his gaze from the valley to the construction site behind them. He visualized the house he'd designed there, remembering the excitement he'd felt as he worked on it, the satisfaction he'd felt sitting before his laptop as it all came together. "I'm considering taking a position at headquarters after I finish in Dubai."

Aidan frowned. "A desk job?"

"Yes."

"You'll hate it," his friend commented.

"I can't travel the globe forever, at least, not if I ever want to settle down. Wife. Kids."

"Is that what you want?" Aidan asked.

"I don't know," Flynn told him honestly. It wasn't something he'd ever spent any time thinking about, at least, not until he'd met Ruby.

"It's the American, isn't it? The one you few to Paris to be with?" Aidan turned to stare at him. "You've fallen in love."

Flynn rocked back on his heels, swallowing his automatic rejection of Aidan's words, because...because he couldn't get Ruby out of his head, hadn't truly been happy since he'd left her, couldn't seem to envision any kind of future that didn't include her. "I think maybe I have."

"And you're considering taking a desk job at Exeter for her?"

"Perhaps."

"Is that what she wants?" Aidan asked.

"No." It was his mother who'd put this thought into his head, not Ruby.

"What does she want, then?"

"She just wants me to be happy," he said quietly, remembering how she'd encouraged him to pursue his dreams, to find his own path the way she'd done. *Stop holding yourself back*, she'd told him that afternoon in Paris. "I'll submit a bid for your friend's project."

"Is that all?" Aidan asked, cutting a glance in his direction.

"No, it's not all." Flynn turned abruptly to face his friend's future home site. "Ruby was right. I should be doing this full-time. I *could* be doing this full-time instead of making myself miserable trying to fulfill a family obligation at Exeter."

"Now you're talking." Aidan grinned at him. "Anything else?"

"Yeah. I'm going to need to cancel our dinner plans for the evening."

"Any particular reason?" Aidan asked with a knowing smile.

"I've got to book a flight to America."

RUBY SAT ON THE BENCH OVERLOOKING ROSEMONT CASTLE, THE same bench where she'd told Flynn she was falling in love with him and he'd told her he couldn't stay. Today, she'd brought her laptop and a picnic for one, yearning for a little peace and solitude as she worked. The air was a crisp sixty-five degrees, perfect inside her purple fleece jacket.

She wore fingerless gloves to keep her hands warm as she

typed, and she was halfway through today's to-do list by the time she decided to pull out the sandwich she'd brought with her. Maybe she should come up here every day to work. Not only was it ridiculously peaceful, but without internet access, her productivity had increased to a ridiculous level.

She'd just taken a huge bite out of her sandwich when she heard footsteps crunching in the leaves behind her. A deer? She turned quietly, hoping not to startle it away. She loved when she stumbled across wildlife out here—or when wildlife stumbled across her. But there was no deer in the woods behind her, and actually, these footsteps sounded human. Probably one of the castle's guests out for a hike.

She chewed and swallowed so she wouldn't be caught with a mouthful, reaching for her water to wash it down. And then the bottle slipped from her fingers, landing in the leaf bed at her feet with a muffled thump.

Flynn stood in front of her on the path, wearing jeans and a forest green pullover jacket, his wavy brown hair as disreputably tousled as ever. She stood, facing him, blinking like an owl behind her glasses because...was he really here? *Why* was he here?

"Hi," he said quietly.

"Hi."

"Elle told me I'd find you here."

She nodded, her throat gone tight. "Yes, I told her where to find me. But why are *you* here?"

He took a step closer. "I'm on my way to Dubai."

"And Virginia happened to be on your way?" But her brain had already formed an image of the globe, and Virginia was in the opposite direction of Dubai from London.

"In a matter of speaking. I needed to see you," he said, his tone earnest.

"Okay." Her heart fluttered like one of the birds in the trees overhead, because her slightly frantic brain couldn't think of a reason for him to be standing in front of her right now that she didn't like.

"Did a lot of thinking after I left here last week," he said.

"Oh?"

He nodded. "And I've decided to leave Exeter. I told my parents yesterday."

"Oh," she repeated, her voice little more than a whisper.

"I'm going to open my own architectural firm, like you suggested." He walked forward, gesturing for her to sit beside him on the bench, which was convenient because her knees were about to give out anyway. "You helped me see what I hadn't noticed before, how much happier and more fulfilled I am when I'm working for myself, when I'm creating my own designs instead of conforming to a corporate brand."

"I'm so glad," she breathed. "And how did your parents take it?"

"Surprisingly well," he told her. "They knew I wasn't happy, and if this new venture finally helps me achieve that, they're in full support."

"Good," she said, reaching over to cover his hand with hers. "I'm so glad, Flynn."

"I still have to go to Dubai, but it'll be my last assignment with Exeter."

She nodded. "That makes sense."

"I'll still travel, depending on where my clients are located, but this should allow me to live a more settled lifestyle." He looked over at her with a wry smile. "As settled as I'm ever likely to get."

She smiled back. "I like it."

"If you're willing, I thought maybe we could redo the conversation we had here last week?" His brown eyes locked on hers, so earnest—*vulnerable*—that she could hardly breathe. Everything inside her chest felt too warm, too tight, like she might burst from the strength of her own emotions.

"Okay," she whispered. "But this time, you lead." Because

she'd already laid her heart out for him, and now it was his turn.

"Fair enough," he agreed. "Ruby Keller, I had no idea how my life was going to change the night I pulled you out of a rosebush on the Langdon estate."

She grinned at the memory. They'd sat on a bench together that night too, and he'd helped her remove all the pins from her hair to get the thorns out before pinning it back up for her.

"The funniest thing happened after I met you." He flipped their hands, giving hers a squeeze. "I felt...peaceful when we were together. I'd never really felt that before. It's like, when I'm with you, everything just makes sense."

"Oh." Tears spilled over her eyelids, and she pushed her glasses up to wipe them away.

"You helped me realize what I want out of life, for my career, and for my heart. And Ruby, I'm falling in love with you too."

"Oh my God." She pressed her hands against her eyes, glasses tumbling into the leaves at her feet.

He picked them up, tapping her on the shoulder. "Put these back on so you can see me, because I just realized it's not exactly true that I'm falling in love with you."

"No?" She slid the glasses into place, blinking away tears to meet his gaze.

"I'm already in love with you. One hundred percent." He leaned in, hands tugging at the clasp on the back of her head so her hair tumbled down her back as their lips met.

"Me too," she whispered, tears sliding over her cheeks and fogging her glasses. "I'm so in love with you, Flynn."

"I can't promise you much these next few months," he said. "I'll be half a world away, but I'll visit you every chance I get, and maybe you can fly over and visit me too."

"I'd love that."

"And after that, maybe we can design a house to live in together. Here, or in London."

"Or both," she said, smiling through her tears. "We should have both."

"Yes. I like that." He wrapped his arms around her, pulling her flush with the warmth of his body. "Both. Anything. Everything. We should have it all."

"I think we will," she said. "Because all we really need is each other."

"I love you." His fingers tangled in her hair as he drew her in for another kiss, this one deeper and hungrier than the last.

"Love you too." She slid into his lap, straddling him. "When I met you, I was about to embark on this adventure that scared the crap out of me. I thought it was going to be about letting go of my inhibitions and flying blind, but I realized I already had that in me. Instead, my adventure was finding you. And I can't wait to see what we discover next."

EPILOGUE

Six Months Later

*R*uby stood on the tarmac at the Towering Pines Regional Airport, one hip leaned against the Bentley. Two years ago, she'd have laughed her ass off at the idea of herself waiting for a private jet to land, leaning against the car she'd been driven here from Rosemont Castle in, by her own personal driver. Well, James wasn't *her* driver. But close enough. How much her life had changed since she, Elle, and Megan entered *Modern Home and Gardens'* Almost Royal contest...

In the distance, a gray shape took form in the sky, its shape rippling in the heat rising off the asphalt. The airplane had its landing gear down, swooping toward them, and her stomach swooped right along with it in anticipation of seeing the man she loved. She watched as the jet lined itself up with the end of the runway and touched down with a roar of the engines.

The plane turned, taxiing toward the terminal, and Ruby sank her weight into her heels, fighting the urge to rush toward it, to climb aboard, to see him. After what felt like an eternity, it came to a stop not far from where she stood, still leaned against the Bentley. She waited until the rolling staircase had been attached and the door opened before she finally stepped forward.

By now, she knew the drill. And by the time she'd reached the plane, Flynn was walking down the steps. She broke into a run, slamming into him in her excitement. His arms came around her, and he spun her around, kissing her as her feet left the ground.

"Hi," he murmured against her lips, eyes crinkled from the smile that had overtaken his face.

"Hi." She wrapped her arms even more tightly around him, because this time, she didn't have to let him go. This time, he was home to stay.

He set her down, holding her at arms' length while he took her in. "You cut your hair." His tone raised in surprise.

"I did. Do you like it?"

"Let me see." He drew her in for another kiss, one hand finding its way into the depths of her newly short hair. He'd always done this. Usually, he would tug the clip out of her hair to free it from its confines, letting it tumble down her back. Today, he tugged lightly at it as his fingers slipped easily through the short strands. "Yes, I do. I love it, in fact."

"I'm glad." She smiled up at him.

"Always did think it was a shame to have all that hair if you never let it down."

"You were right."

He gave her another searching look, hands still buried in her hair. "It suits you."

"And it's a lot lighter."

"I missed you." He pressed his forehead against hers, hands sliding down to grip her waist, anchoring them together.

"Me too." They held each other like that for a long minute,

just breathing in the comfort that came from being together. "What do you say we go home?"

"I'd love to."

They walked to the Bentley and climbed inside. James had already loaded Flynn's luggage, and he began driving toward Rosemont Castle. For today, they were headed for the guest house, but now that Flynn was back, they could begin building their real home together. Last month, he had bought a parcel of land adjacent to Rosemont Castle, and they'd already started discussing what kind of house they wanted to put on it.

They would live primarily here in Virginia while he got his newly formed architectural firm up and running, but he still had his flat in London too, and as most of his current clients were in the UK, they'd probably spend a lot of time there. Ruby didn't mind. She'd fallen in love with London the first time she visited and couldn't wait to go back.

By the time the Bentley rolled down the castle's winding drive, she and Flynn were already kissing, leaned in across the backseat, a desperation born out of not having seen each other since she flew to Dubai for a quick visit over a month ago. They thanked James for driving them, got Flynn's bags out of the trunk, and hurried inside.

"God, I need you." He pressed her against the wall, hands cupping her face as his lips met hers. "I missed you so damn much."

"Same. Oh," she gasped as he shoved one of his thighs between her legs so that she was straddling him.

"I think I need to explore this new hairdo more intimately." He gave her hair another light tug before lifting her into his arms and carrying her down the hall toward the bedroom.

～

TWO HOURS LATER, THEY MADE THEIR WAY UP TO THE CASTLE FOR

dinner. Ruby had changed into a multi-colored wrap skirt and a red top. Her hair blew in the spring breeze, light and carefree.

"Really love this." Flynn reached out to tuck a strand of it behind her ear.

"Me too." She leaned in to kiss him as they climbed the castle's front steps. Inside, they followed the sound of Elle and Theo's voices to the kitchen, where they found them engaged in a good-natured argument over whether or not the Fairy Tails Ball should become an annual tradition.

"Well, we've hosted it the past two years, so I think continuing the tradition is a no-brainer," Elle was saying. "Oh, hi guys! Welcome back, Flynn."

In between hellos, Ruby threw in her support for the Fairy Tails Ball, and Theo raised his hands in defeat. "Fine, fine, as long as I have no part in planning it."

Elle rolled her eyes. "You've never had a part in planning it. Leave that to us. You just show up and look pretty."

"That part I can definitely handle." He leaned in to kiss his wife as Ruby and Flynn watched in amusement.

"Did we miss anything?" Megan appeared in the doorway with Jake at her side.

"Couldn't get her off the computer," Jake said with a smile. "She's become obsessed with honeymoon plans. If you ask me, she's more excited about the honeymoon than the wedding."

"Hey." Megan jabbed a finger into his chest. "I resent that."

It had been over a month now since they got engaged, and Megan hadn't stopped talking about wedding—or honeymoon—plans since. Ruby just shook her head. They'd jumped straight from Elle's wedding into planning Megan's. A pattern Ruby hoped might continue once she and Flynn were settled in their new home together.

They moved into the dining room for dinner, vegetable lasagna, salad, and garlic bread. Flynn entertained everyone with details of the new hotel in Dubai, which had celebrated its grand opening yesterday, before Megan told them about the private beachfront villas on Grand Cayman she'd decided would be the perfect honeymoon destination.

"Do you realize how far we've all come in two years?" Elle said, looking around the table with a dreamy expression on her face. "I don't mean to be sappy, but my life was a hot mess when I got that call from the magazine telling us we'd won the contest."

"And to be honest, I thought the contest was going to turn out to be a hoax," Ruby said. "I mean, what kind of real-life earl would give away the chance to manage his castle in a magazine?"

"And what kind of earl has a castle in Virginia?" Megan added, laughter dancing in her eyes.

"I thought we'd come, play around for a few weeks, and go back home to Florida," Ruby admitted.

"I did too," Megan said.

"And you two tried so hard to get me to give up and leave." Elle narrowed her eyes at them. "Imagine if I hadn't fought for the chance to stay? If we'd just gone home when Theo tried to kick us out?"

"I didn't try to kick you out," Theo said, eyebrows raised. "Although I did try to buy you out."

"Same thing," Megan told him with a grin. "Elle's right. We showed up here with nothing but a couple of suitcases and big dreams."

"I never imagined it would all turn out like this. I *married* the earl." Elle's chest shook with laughter. "And Megan found Jake, and now Ruby's got Flynn. It's all just too good to be true, isn't it?"

"No," Jake said, reaching over to squeeze his fiancée's hand. "I don't think anything's ever too good to be true."

"Aww." Megan leaned over to kiss him.

After dinner, Ruby and Flynn headed for the guest house. She could hardly wait to continue their reunion...in bed. But Flynn tugged her hand, guiding her toward the gardens in front of the castle, heavily in bloom, now that spring had arrived.

"Let's go for a little walk before we turn in for the night," he said. "I need to stretch my legs after the long flight."

"Okay," she agreed, walking beside him down the gravel path.

"This reminds me of the night we met." He reached out to touch a rosebush. "Another garden, another continent, another Langdon property, and here we are."

"Here we are," she echoed. "See that fountain? Theo's grandparents renewed their vows there fifty years ago. Theo proposed to Elle right there too."

"Did he?" Flynn looked over at her, something unreadable shining in his eyes.

"Yep."

"I'm partial to rosebushes myself." He led her down a path to the left, lined with roses in every color, muted now by the twilight around them.

"Favorite color?" she asked.

"Ruby red, of course." He plucked one and held it toward her. "I confess, I did have an ulterior motive for bringing you into the garden tonight."

"You did?" Her breath caught in her throat as she took the rose. She brought it to her nose, inhaling its rich scent as her eyes locked on his.

"I did. In fact, I did a lot of thinking during these last few months in Dubai, about you, and me, and our future together. About how lucky I was when I found you in that garden in London last fall."

"Oh." Her heart beat against her ribs, the scent of the rose making her almost dizzy with anticipation.

Flynn was looking at her like she was a fairytale princess, and he was her prince. And this was the part at the end of the movie where...

He dropped to one knee, pulling out a black velvet box

from his pants pocket. "Ruby Keller, would you do me the incredible honor of agreeing to be my wife?"

"Yes...yes, yes, yes!" She pressed a hand against her chest, the rose falling to the gravel at her feet.

"Phew." He grinned up at her. "That was nerve-wracking."

"As if I would say no. Oh..." She caught sight of the diamond ring in his hand, and her pulse skyrocketed. This was really happening. *Oh my God.* "Flynn, it's so beautiful."

"I thought about getting you one with rubies in it, but I decided it might be cliché." He slid the ring onto her finger, and they both stared at it for a moment in awed silence. "Wow, my ring on your finger looks even more amazing than I could have imagined."

"Get up here so I can kiss you." She tugged at his hand, and he stood.

They wound their arms around each other, kissing desperately. Tears blurred her vision, fogging her glasses, and she swiped at them impatiently so she could see her hand pressed against Flynn's chest, the diamond sparkling on her finger. "It's perfect."

"You're perfect." He kissed her again.

"Should we go back in and tell them?" she asked with a smile, tipping her head toward the castle.

"If you want to elicit a lot of screaming and hugging," he said with a grin.

"Let's do it," she whispered. "It's the perfect end to a perfect night. And then I'll take you down to the guest house so we can celebrate in private."

"And *that* sounds like a perfect ending to me."

DEAR READER,

I hope you enjoyed *Let Your Hair Down*! This was such a fun book to write, and as luck would have it, I got to take a trip to London and Paris earlier this year that mirrored a lot of Ruby's journey. If you missed either of the first two books in the series, you can go back and see Elle and Theo fall in love in *If the Shoe Fits* (Almost Royal #1), and Megan and Jake in *Once Upon a Cowboy* (Almost Royal #2).

Sign up for my newsletter for exclusive news and giveaways and receive a free copy of my award-winning novella, *Only You*, just for subscribing. If you enjoy chatting about books, I'd love for you to join my reader group on Facebook. It's a great place for us to stay in touch, and I often ask for help naming upcoming characters and pets plus lots of other fun reader group exclusives.

Hope to see you there!
Rachel Lacey

NEWSLETTER SIGNUP

Make sure you sign up for my newsletter! You'll receive a FREE novella just for joining and first looks at everything I'm working on.

http://www.subscribepage.com/rachellaceyauthor

ACKNOWLEDGMENTS

Thank you so much to my agent, Sarah Younger, and the rest of the NYLA team for all your help with *Let Your Hair Down*. And of course, a huge thank you to my always amazing critique partner, Annie Rains, for guiding me in the right direction.

Special thanks to the lovely Mia Sosa for naming Exeter Hotels and Resorts.

A huge thank you to all the readers, bloggers, and reviewers who've read my books and supported me along the way. Love you all!

xx

Rachel

IF THE SHOE FITS EXCERPT

Elle Davenport tugged at the bodice of her ball gown where the ribbing poked into her skin. When she'd been a little girl dreaming about fairytale princesses, she'd had no idea the dresses would be so uncomfortable. Of course, real-life princesses probably had gowns made of super-soft silk, unlike Elle's theme park knock-off.

She continued down the sidewalk, waving at a group of children waiting in line for popcorn, her skirt swooshing around her feet as she walked. The Florida sun blazed overhead, and she glanced at the clock tower to her left. Ten minutes until her break...

"Princess Ariana!" A little girl ran toward her, arms outstretched.

Elle knelt and gathered her in for a hug. "Hi there, sweetie. What's your name?"

"Britney," the girl told her. "You're just as beautiful in real life, Princess Ariana."

"Aw, thank you, Britney. That's so sweet of you to say." As hot and uncomfortable as she was, moments like this one made her job worthwhile. Dressing up as a theme park princess wasn't at all what she'd planned to be doing at twenty-five, but it wasn't the worst job she'd ever had either. She signed Britney's autograph book and posed with her while the girl's parents took several photos before the family continued on their way.

Elle greeted a few more guests and then headed up the steps of the welcome center, eager for fifteen minutes of air conditioning. She lifted her skirt to keep from tripping over it, smiling as she saw her gold Gucci sandals peeking out from beneath its red satin folds. Her dress might have been uncomfortable, but her shoes sure weren't. Shoes were her one splurge, and this pair—with colorful flowers embroidered across the top strap—made her feel like a real princess.

She ducked down the hall to the employee break room and filled a cup of water from the cooler. As she took a grateful sip, her cell phone started ringing from inside her locker. She fumbled to open it, grabbing her phone from the depths of her purse. The number came up with a 212 area code which—thanks to that one year after high school when she'd decided to try her luck with acting—she remembered was a New York City exchange. Acting had been a bust, though, and she didn't know anyone in New York City.

Still, something compelled her to press the phone to her ear instead of letting it go to voicemail. "Hello?"

"Am I speaking with Elle Davenport?" a female voice asked.

"Yes. Who's this?" Elle smoothed her free hand over the perfectly coifed blonde wig she wore. She was a natural blonde, but Princess Ariana's hairdo was intricate, and it just wasn't practical to spend hours getting her hair done every morning before work.

"My name is Monica Jackson, and I'm the outreach coordinator at *Modern Home and Gardens* magazine."

"*Modern Home and Gardens*," Elle repeated as her brain clicked up to speed because *holy shit*, memories of a wine-infused girls' night danced behind her eyelids. That night, after a few bottles of wine and a lot of laughter, she and her friends had entered the most outrageous contest…

"That's right," Monica said. "You entered our Almost Royal contest, and I'm so pleased to tell you that, after careful consideration, you and your co-applicants Ruby Keller and Megan Perl have been chosen as our winners."

"Wait—what?" Elle pressed a hand to her forehead. She never won stuff, and this…this was by far the biggest contest she'd ever entered.

"You won!" Monica repeated with a laugh. "If you accept, you'll be moving into Rosemont Castle in Towering Pines, Virginia, for a period of six months, during which time you'll have the opportunity to put the ideas you proposed in your entry essay into practice. I have to say, our team *loved* your 'Fairy Tails' concept where guests at the castle visit with adoptable animals during their stay."

"Holy crap." Elle sounded like she'd swallowed helium, and she didn't even care. That last part had been Ruby's idea—for guests to have the opportunity to meet and hopefully fall in love with their own furry Prince or Princess Charming while they stayed at Rosemont Castle. Elle had thought it a bit much, but if this was what had won the contest for them, she would never doubt her nerdy, rescue-pet-loving friend again.

"You'll be compensated for your work, of course," Monica said. "The owners of the castle—the Langdon family—have stipulated generous monthly salaries for you, and all business expenses will be covered. At the end of the six-month period, they will evaluate your work and decide whether to keep you on to manage the property for them. If your venture is profitable, there is potential for your position to become permanent."

"That's…that's amazing." Elle knew she should have something more eloquent to say, but her mind was tumbling in a million different directions. She, Megan, and Ruby were going to move into a castle, a real-life castle owned by relatives of the

British royal family. She danced on the spot, her ball gown swirling around her ankles, and hey, at least she was dressed for the occasion. She choked back a laugh.

"Now we realize that a lot of people entered this contest with no real expectation of winning," Monica continued. "To accept your prize, you'll need to move to Virginia for a minimum of six months and live and work at Rosemont Castle, which will culminate in a spread in *Modern Home and Gardens'* January issue detailing your time and work there. This is a big commitment, so we urge you to let us know as soon as possible if you'll be unable to fulfill your obligations."

It was true that Elle and her friends had entered the contest without expecting to win. Truthfully, she hadn't given it a second thought since the night they'd sent in their essay. But there was *no way* she was passing up this opportunity, and she knew her friends would say the same thing. "Oh, we're in. We are definitely in."

And that was how, three weeks later, Elle found herself riding in a shiny black limousine through the Virginia country-side with her best friends. She pressed her nose against the glass like an excited child as the limo wound its way down the endless paved driveway leading to Rosemont Castle. Tall trees rose on either side of them, forming a green canopy overhead. After twenty-five years in Florida, she felt out of place here in the middle of the Appalachian Mountains. She might feel lost right now, but she hoped to find something wonderful at the end of this drive. Maybe even life-changing.

The stakes for today were impossibly high. She and her friends had quit their jobs and moved out of their apartments for this opportunity. What if they messed up and the Langdon family sent them packing? She sat up straighter in her seat. She'd just have to work extra hard during their time here to make sure that didn't happen.

"I see something," Megan said beside her.

"Where?" Elle peered through the window, her heart accelerating the way she wished the limo would, but it kept up its steady crawl along the winding driveway.

"All I see are trees," Ruby said, keeping one hand firmly on the cat carrier in front of her.

"There!" Megan called, and sure enough, Elle caught a glimpse of a stone structure through the trees.

Rosemont Castle. This was really happening.

The limo rounded a bend, and the castle came into full view. It looked like something straight out of her childhood fairytales, with an elaborate façade built from stone bricks, a tall tower on one side, and a huge fountain splashing from the middle of the circular drive. There were lush gardens to the left and rolling hills as far as she could see, scattered with various outbuildings.

"It looks just like it did in the photographs," Ruby said. "Except bigger."

"Definitely bigger." Even Megan sounded awestruck.

Elle pressed a hand to her chest. She'd always thought the expression was just a cliché, but right now she literally felt like she'd had her breath taken away. From her one-bedroom apartment in Orlando to this? Happiness bloomed inside her, as vibrant as the flowers lining the driveway.

According to their contact at the magazine, the castle's owner, Alistair Langdon, the Earl of Highcastle aka an actual relative of the British Monarchy, had passed away recently. The rest of the Langdons lived in England, so Elle and her friends should have pretty much free rein over Rosemont Castle for the duration of their stay.

If they were successful in finding a way for the castle to pay for its own upkeep, the Langdon family had the option to keep Elle, Megan, and Ruby on site indefinitely as property managers, and that's exactly what Elle was counting on. This was her fresh start in life—a fresh start of royal proportions.

Nothing was going to mess it up.

The limo pulled into the circular drive, slowing to a stop in front of the castle's dramatic front steps. The driver came around and opened the door for them. Ruby got out first, a cat carrier in each hand. Megan followed, with Elle bringing up the rear.

She stepped out of the limo and stood staring up at the castle. It was even more impressive now than it had been from inside the limo, standing picturesque against the bright blue sky. The sound of water splashing into fountains reached her ears. The air was cool and fresh, impossibly fresh. She sucked in a deep breath, a wide smile spreading across her face.

An elderly man in a crisp black uniform and white gloves came down the front steps. "Good afternoon. You must be Miss Davenport, Miss Perl, and Miss Keller." He spoke with a British accent, and if he was an actual English butler, Elle might faint on the spot.

"Yes, we are," Megan replied with an eager smile, her brown hair blowing in the breeze.

"Welcome to Rosemont Castle," he said briskly. "My name is Colin, and I'm the butler here. If you would like to follow me, I will show you in and have your luggage brought inside."

"That sounds lovely," Megan told him, still beaming.

Elle seemed to have lost her tongue. Her brain had gone fuzzy. A castle with a butler. How was this her real life? By now, the limo driver had lined up all their luggage on the asphalt beside them. She followed Megan and Ruby up the stone steps toward the castle's entrance.

As she reached the top step, one of Ruby's cat carriers bumped into her shin. Elle stumbled off balance, and her rhinestone-encrusted sandal (she'd worked very hard on her first-day-in-a-castle outfit, thank you very much!) slipped from her foot and tumbled down the steps behind her with a clatter.

Well, that was an embarrassing way to make an entrance.

She turned, uneven now in one kitten-heeled sandal and one bare foot. A man stood at the bottom of the steps, holding her sandal and staring up at her with piercing blue eyes. His black hair was almost long enough to reach his collar, thick and wavy. He wore a powder-blue polo shirt and khaki shorts, and *hello*, he was gorgeous. And he must think she was a total klutz. She swallowed hard.

He held up her shoe. "I believe this belongs to you?"

~

Theo Langdon climbed the steps to hand the pretty blonde her shoe. These must be the winners of the magazine contest, and as irritated as he was by the situation, he couldn't help but admire the women on his front steps. They were all pretty, but he couldn't tear his gaze away from the blonde.

Her hair tumbled over her shoulders in loose curls that were pinned back from her face on one side. She wore a light pink dress with thin straps that showed off her toned and tanned shoulders and a white belt that accentuated her waist. She wobbled as she bent to slide the runaway shoe back onto her foot, and he held out a hand to steady her. Her hand was warm and delicate in his.

She straightened to face him, her cheeks flushed nearly as pink as her dress. "Thank you. I'm Elle Davenport."

"Theo Langdon." He watched as her green eyes widened.

"Oh! You're one of the Langdons."

He nodded. "That's right."

"We're so thrilled to be here, Mr. Langdon," one of Elle's friends said, extending her hand with a wide smile. "This is a dream come true for us."

"You can call me Theo." As the newly appointed Earl of Highcastle, they should technically address him as "my lord," but he'd never been big on formalities, especially not here in America. And anyway, he was still coming to terms with the fact that the title no longer belonged to his grandfather. Alistair's death had come as a shock to everyone, but especially to Theo.

"I'm Megan." She gave his hand a firm shake. "And that's Ruby."

Ruby, whose glasses and tight bun reminded him of a younger version of his high school English teacher, gave him a shy nod. A cat carrier sat on either side of her, and two sets of feline eyes gleamed up at him from within them.

"Pleasure to meet you ladies," he said. If they'd met under different circumstances, it really would be a pleasure. He would have enjoyed getting to know them—especially Elle—but right now, their presence was an unwanted complication. He very much needed to get Rosemont Castle sorted out and sold so that he could return to London before the end of the summer.

"We, ah, we were under the impression you lived in England," Elle said, still watching him closely.

"Hoping to have the place to yourselves, were you?"

"Oh, no, not at all," she stammered.

He fought a smile. "I do live in London, but I'll be here for the time being while I wrap up my grandfather's affairs."

"Of course."

"In fact, I was hoping to go over some business with you ladies, if you don't mind?" He'd purposefully caught them on their way in so he could break his news before they'd had a chance to get attached to the castle.

"Okay." Elle held him in her steady, green-eyed stare.

"I'll just take a few minutes of your time, and then you can get settled in." He motioned for them to follow him inside, but as he did so, his cell phone began to ring. He swiped it from his pocket and saw the number for the London office displayed on the screen. Reluctantly, he shifted gears. "Actually, I need to take this. Have Colin find me once you're settled, and we'll talk then."

He pushed through the castle's heavy wooden doors, connecting the call as he walked.

"Theo." His uncle George Langdon's voice boomed over the

line. "Our board members have been asking after you. How long until you're back in London?"

He started down the hall toward his office. "I hope to have everything wrapped up here in the next few weeks."

"We're counting on you, my boy."

Theo understood his uncle's meaning perfectly. The family had long scorned his grandfather's decision to live primarily in America. They felt he'd neglected his duties as the Earl of Highcastle. Now that Theo had inherited the title, they expected him to step up in the ways his grandfather had not. "There are a few matters here that have to be dealt with, but I'll be back in London as soon as possible."

"Don't forget about the Gardener charity event on the twentieth of June," his uncle said.

"I'll be there."

Elle stepped inside the castle's front doors and stopped there to take it all in. The foyer was two stories high, with vaulted ceilings and huge windows that let in lots of natural light. Polished marble floors glistened beneath her feet, and an ornate crystal chandelier twinkled overhead. To her left, a wooden staircase curved upward toward the second floor.

"You'll find the available guest bedrooms up those stairs," Colin told them. "The Langdons' private quarters are in the rear of the castle and have been closed off. Once you have selected your rooms, I will have your luggage brought up."

"Thank you," Megan said as she began to climb the staircase.

A high-pitched wail echoed around the foyer as one of Ruby's cats expressed his dismay at the long journey. "Just a few more minutes, Simon," she said as she bent next to his carrier. "Let me pick out our room, and then you can come out of there."

Elle jogged up the stairs after Megan and Ruby. "You guys, I feel like I'm on a movie set or something right now."

"It's surreal, all right," Ruby said as they reached the top of the stairs. "Should we check out the rooms together before we decide?"

"Sounds like a plan to me." Megan was already walking down the hallway ahead.

The first room they came to had a king-sized bed with a navy blue bedspread and an ornately-carved head and foot-board that matched the rest of the furniture in the room. Megan twirled an imaginary skirt, batting her eyelashes like a cartoon princess as she danced her way across the room.

Ruby snorted with laughter.

"We should keep in mind which rooms would make the best guest rooms," Elle said with a grin as she walked to the window and took in the sweeping views of the grounds below. A big part of their plan for Rosemont Castle involved opening some of its many bedrooms to guests looking for a "royal" vacation getaway.

"That's right," Ruby said with a nod as she surveyed the room. "Which means we should look for out-of-the-way rooms and save ones like this for our guests."

"So this is a guest room. That was easy." Megan led the way back into the hall.

They wandered up and down the hallways, familiarizing themselves with the twelve—yes, twelve—available bedrooms on the East and West wings of the castle. All were decorated with a classic touch, some in earth tones, others in brighter colors.

Elle ran her fingers over yet another intricately-carved headboard. "Do you think this is a Langdon piece?" In her research on the family, she'd learned that they owned Langdon Fine Furnishings, one of the top producers of handcrafted furniture in Europe. Its charitable division—the Langdon Family Foundation—provided furnishings and other household goods to families in need throughout the United Kingdom.

"It would make sense," Ruby said. "Now that you mention it, I can't imagine Alistair Langdon having anyone's furniture in this house but his own."

"It could be another selling point," Elle said as she followed them out of the room. "If a guest likes something they see in their room, they can go home and order it for themselves."

"I'm not so sure they can." Ruby grasped the handle on a door at the end of the hall. "I think Langdon Fine Furnishings is only available in Europe. I wonder what's through here?" She pushed it open, revealing yet another hallway containing three bedrooms. These rooms were smaller and overlooked the wooded area behind the castle.

"I think we've found our rooms," Elle said as she peeked inside the first one, decorated a sunny yellow. It was bright and happy and easily her favorite room that they'd seen so far.

"They're perfect," Megan agreed as she walked into the bedroom next door. It had a brightly-colored quilt striped with shades of red and burgundy, soft pink walls, and an oversized window with sheer curtains.

Ruby crossed the hall and opened another door. It revealed a spiral stone staircase which led to both upper and lower floors. Eyebrows raised, Ruby gave Elle and Megan a look as she started up. Elle grinned as she hurried after her. About halfway up the stairs, Elle peeked out one of the windows and gasped. "You guys, we're in the tower!"

"You're right." Ruby picked up the pace, hurrying toward the doorway at the top of the stairs. She opened it, revealing a rounded bedroom inside. The room was bright with off-white walls and a cushioned ledge running around its perimeter, making one never-ending reading nook in front of the over-sized windows. A day bed sat along the far wall, with white-painted wrought iron rails and a bedspread decorated with colorful butterflies. "Dibs," Ruby said, as a smile spread slowly across her face.

"What? No fair!" Megan walked to the window. "Holy crap, the view is amazing."

"I need more space because I'll have Simon and Oliver in the room with me."

"Can you believe her?" Megan asked Elle with an amused grin. "She wants a bigger room because of her cats."

Elle held her hands out in front of herself. "I want the yellow bedroom downstairs, so this is totally between you guys."

"Please?" Ruby asked with a sweet smile.

"Oh, fine," Megan acquiesced. "That daybed is too small for me anyway. I'd rather have the bigger bed downstairs."

"You're the best." Ruby gave her a quick hug. "I'm going to get the cats set up in here and then we can finish exploring."

Elle walked back down the stairs to get a closer look at her new room. She swept her hand across the soft bedspread and walked to the window. Her room overlooked the rolling hills and thick woods of the Appalachian Mountains, and this view might be even more enchanting than the picturesque gardens visible from the front of the castle. Once they were all settled in, she wanted to go exploring in those woods too.

A plush chair sat by the window, and Elle could already imagine herself curled up there with a book and maybe a little dog in her lap. After a half dozen false starts since she made the decision to pursue acting instead of college, she finally, *finally* felt like she was headed in the right direction with her life.

"Ready to go exploring?" Ruby said from the doorway.

Megan appeared beside her. "I know I am."

"So ready." Elle followed them downstairs.

Colin was waiting for them, and they let him know which bedrooms they'd picked out. With that taken care of, they headed for the front door, laughing and chatting excitedly, eager to explore the castle's grounds.

The heavy front door opened before they'd reached it, and Theo Langdon stood silhouetted against the late afternoon sun. It filtered through his dark hair, giving him a sort of golden aura, and Elle's heart skittered in her chest. Okay, so the man was seriously hot, and he spoke with just a hint of a British accent that was ridiculously sexy.

But he was also her landlord, and yeah…not going there. She'd ruined enough things in her life already. No way was she going to risk the best thing that had ever happened to her by lusting after a man who was practically her boss.

"Could I have a moment?" he asked, addressing the three of them. Maybe it was Elle's imagination, but his gaze seemed to linger a moment longer on her.

Her cheeks grew warm. "Of course."

He led the way down the hall. Elle followed, surreptitiously glancing into every room they passed. She saw a lounge with plush seating and a baby grand piano and caught a glimpse of a library that was absolutely to-die-for before Theo led them into what appeared to be his office, motioning them toward a circular wooden table just large enough for the four of them.

Once Elle, Ruby, and Megan had followed him in, he shut the door behind them. "I have some business to discuss with you ladies."

Elle sat in the chair across from him. "Should I get my laptop?"

"That won't be necessary," he said.

Ruby and Megan settled into the two remaining seats at the table.

"We'd love to go over the details of our business plan with you," Megan said, her brown eyes sparkling. "We've done a lot of planning since finding out we won the contest, and we have some really exciting ideas for bringing income into the castle."

"That's not exactly what I brought you in here to discuss," Theo said, and something in his tone made Elle sit up straighter in her seat.

"As you know, my grandfather passed away recently," Theo said. "He built this castle fifty years ago when he fell in love with my grandmother, Rose. She was an American, and they lived here pretty much full time. Now that they're both gone, the family has decided that it would be in our best interest to sell Rosemont Castle."

ABOUT THE AUTHOR

 Rachel Lacey is a contemporary romance author and semi-reformed travel junkie. She's been climbed by a monkey on a mountain in Japan, gone scuba diving on the Great Barrier Reef, and camped out overnight in New York City for a chance to be an extra in a movie. These days, the majority of her adventures take place on the pages of the books she writes. She lives in warm and sunny North Carolina with her husband, son, and a variety of rescue pets.

f facebook.com/RachelLaceyAuthor

🐦 twitter.com/rachelslacey

instagram.com/rachelslacey

a amazon.com/author/rachellacey

BB bookbub.com/authors/rachel-lacey

CPSIA information can be obtained
at www.ICGtesting.com
Printed in the USA
LVHW111515121219
640280LV00003B/441/P